Urban Fairytales

A COLLECTION OF GROWN FOLKS STORIES

Donna Fair

Donna Fair
1/20/07

SaySo Publishing

Urban fairytales: A collection of grown folks stories / Donna Fair

Manufactured in the United States of America

First Edition

Cover design by Mischa Green

SaySo Publishing Co.
P.O. Box 1301
Columbia, MD 21044

DEDICATION

This book is dedicated with love to, my parents,

Ellen and Clifton Taylor

who always taught me to "Keep A Goin!";

to my husband, Tony and our boys,

Anthony and Eric

for living my dreams with me.

ACKNOWLEDGEMENTS

I would like to first thank God for taking me on this journey of getting this book published, my husband Tony for giving me excellent advice even when he thought that I wasn't listening, my boys, Anthony and Eric, we all have dreams, please pursue yours as I have pursued one of my own, my father and my sister, Aleta, for always asking how my writing was going, my mother for listening, my friends who pushed me along in getting this book finished, Leslie Stokely, Paula Paolini, Alisa DeGeorge, Dena Narcisse, Sandra Thomas, Barb Collins Jibril, Kamil Jibril and Aden, Kim Lacy Johnson, Dorie Taylor Boone, Deborah Kittrell for lending her reader's eye, Lealie Perry for offering great advice and great business contacts, to those who always gave me feedback when I asked Andrea Crump, Sandy Harris, Nancy Jorcin, Martha Wilhight Cowherd, Alison Ruffino and to Jane Taylor and Natalie Boggs for providing me with encouraging words. I am grateful for the artistic talents of Laura Skidmore and the editing skills of Bobette Watts.

TABLE OF CONTENTS

Erica's Tale

"What is it dat you seek from dis place?" Esther spoke with traces of the patois of her native island. Sister Robinson turned away from her and looked over at the man fidgeting nervously staring at the lotions and oils on the shelf with his back to them. She was checking to see if she recognized him from the church or her neighborhood.

Then she whispered, "I need your help. My husband is cheating on me." Esther raised her hand and slowly removed her sunglasses while staring at Sister Robinson.

"That woman is taking a long time. I gotta grab this stuff and hit the street so I can get my high on," Hector thought to himself standing in front of the shelves. He turned around to see the woman standing at the counter staring right at him. "Damn." He turned back around to face the shelves. A few seconds later, he heard a thud. He turned to find the woman who had just come in passed out on the floor. Esther rushed past him into the back of the store. "Now's my chance," he thought. He grabbed handfuls of oils and stuffed them in his pockets and ran through the door.

Esther held a jar of something reddish brown under Sister Robinson's nose. She grasped for breath as if she were a newborn baby. "Its gwine be alrit," Esther said softly as she helped Sister Robinson sit up on the floor with her back resting against the counter. Then she closed the jar and slipped it into Sister's purse.

"Wait ere," Esther said as she went into the back to get her some water. Sister Robinson had become totally unnerved by the intense power of Esther's eyes penetrating her soul. After a few seconds, she felt a level of confidence that she didn't have before entering the House of Meditation. It must be something in that jar, Sister Robinson thought to herself. When Esther came back with the water, Sister Robinson was gone. There were five twenty-dollar bills stacked on the counter.

Esther laughed to herself. "Yes, dearie, it gwine be alrit."

"Hector, where you going?" his wife Irene asked.

"Baby, daddy is going to find you some rocks laced with gold. Now just go back to sleep, I'll wake you up when the gold is here."

"I want to go with you," she pouted.

"Let me handle this," Hector said as he walked out of the door. He whistled as he walked. He had made some good money on the street selling Esther's healing oils. People didn't come from all over to see her for nothing, he thought to himself. She was well known for her power in soothing a person's mental, physical and emotional state. People saw Esther's symbol on the bottle and that was an instant sell and it wasn't cheap. He needed a new supply. He knew that he had to be careful but his drug addiction was more powerful than his fear. Esther was also known for putting curses on people. Those having problems with their loved ones or others would come ask her to give them a spell that would bring the results they so desired.

As soon as he walked into the dim sunlit House of Meditation, Esther said angrily, "Come ere" pointing her finger at him.

"Who me?" Hector pointed to himself and turned around looking but no one else was in the store. He pimped towards her and stood in front of the counter.

"You steal from me," she said.

"What? Is that how you treat your customers?" He sucked his teeth. "I didn't.....," he stopped in mid sentence.

Esther had removed her sunglasses slowly and placed them on the counter. She stared him straight in the eyes. "You like to play games, huh? Ok den, let's play boy."

Hector dropped to his knees as she continued to stare into his eyes. "Please, please, you're right, I stole from you and I'm sorry. I'll never do it again. Please."

She picked up her sunglasses and put them back on. "I know you won't steal from me no more. Come time for you to pay Esther, eh. Now you shall do something for me," she said. "You will bring me your first born chile."

"What?" Hector said.

"You will give me your first born chile." Esther slapped her hand down hard on the counter. "I will let you live. Now go way from ere. Get out of my sight." Hector scrambled to his feet and ran out the door and down the street. He could hear that crazy woman's laugh for half a block.

Six months later, Hector and Irene went into rehab to clean up their act. One evening, Hector was on his way to his part-time job and he happened past the House of Meditation. Esther appeared in the doorway. "Congratulations!" she yelled at him.

"Huh?" he said as he turned around.

"Your wife, she is with chile." Hector didn't know that Irene was pregnant but he knew if Esther said it was so it was as good as done. "I'll expect the baby come the second Saturday of November." She disappeared from the doorway. Hector had not mentioned the incident with Esther to Irene when it originally happened. At that time, he was so strung out on crack. When he left Esther's that day he just went to another spot in the neighborhood looking for something to steal. However, when Esther told him to bring his first born to her before he or his wife even knew about the pregnancy, he told Irene everything. He knew that he had to give Esther that baby or it was his life and that could mean his wife's life as well.

Irene knew about Esther. She had never been to her personally. However, she knew that Esther wasn't a woman to play with at all. She knew what she had to do. Esther looked at her with her sunglasses on while she stood behind the counter smoking a corncob pipe. Before Irene could speak, Esther said, "I shall name 'er Erica. You and Hector shall bring 'er to me the second Saturday of November."

"Please from one woman to another, allow my husband and I to keep our child," Irene said solemnly.

"Your husband steal from me, gal. Den he lie 'bout it to my face. He must pay for dat wrong he has done."

"Please take anything else just not my baby," she pleaded.

"Hush chile, you must leave, now go!" Irene saw her pleading was to no avail.

"Fine, we'll just run if we need too." She said flippantly as she turned to walk away.

"Gal 'ear dis! Someting you shall know today." Esther raised her hand and Irene instantly froze in her tracks. "You shall now foresee the result of your future if you choose to disobey me." Esther snapped her fingers and Irene was blind. She took a powder from behind the counter and blew it in Irene's direction. Irene couldn't talk. She could hear Esther's haunting laugh ringing in her ears. Suddenly, Esther snapped her fingers twice and Irene could move, see and talk again. She rushed toward the door. "Don't play with me, gal." Esther's haunting laugh rang throughout the store.

Like clockwork, Irene went into labor the second Friday of November. She had a baby girl the next day. Irene and Hector with tears in their eyes took their firstborn to the House of Meditation. Esther was sitting like always behind the counter on her stool smoking her pipe with her sunglasses on and her red, black, green and yellow crocheted tam on her head. Irene and Hector each took turns kissing the baby. Hector sat the baby who was wrapped in a blanket inside a wicker basket on the counter. Irene spoke "I'm coming to you again, one woman to another, please let me keep my baby. I'll do anything as will my husband but please let us keep our firstborn."

Esther calmly picked up the baby basket off of the counter and placed it on the floor behind the counter. Irene cried out loudly "No! Don't take my child." She lunged halfway across the counter.

Hector held her back. Esther slowly took off her sunglasses and sat them on the counter. Hector held onto Irene but turned his eyes away from Esther. She looked directly into Irene's eyes. Irene cried out loudly "No! No!" She looked into Esther's eyes longer than most but at last the bond of motherhood was broken and she had to turn her head away. Hector and Irene left broken and defeated never to return.

True to her word, Esther named the baby, Erica. She kept the baby right beside her behind the counter. Erica was a good baby. She never cried when Esther had customers. She would coo and play with her hands. By the time, she could walk, her beauty was apparent. She had thick curly locks all over her head. Her cheeks were so round that when she smiled she looked like the happiest person on the earth and her eyes. They were sea green. When you looked into them, you immediately felt a sense of comfort feeling all of the love and kindness that she possessed pass right through to you.

Folks noticed the positive effect Erica had on the old Obe woman. They even dared to joke "Least she ain't turned no more mailmen into dogs since she had that child." Everyone had known she didn't get pregnant. But they dare not question her.

Erica never caused any great mischief. If Esther saw her getting into any trouble, she would calmly say, "Come ere little one." Erica would come to her immediately full of happiness and life. And so it remained this way. As she became older, Erica would write and play behind the counter at the House of Meditations. She was always polite to everyone never throwing a tantrum. When she was old enough, Esther began home schooling her. When she was old enough to stay home over the store alone, Esther let her while she herself continued to go to work in the store downstairs.

Esther owned the building that housed the House of Meditation. She had two tenants, Vincent Johnson a.k.a. Ms. Vera and Old man Harris. Both came and went and kept to themselves. They knew all about Esther and therefore, they paid their rent on time and kept their distance.

One evening, Esther came up the back hallway stairs as always. She stopped in front of her doorway and knocked on the door with a secret rhythm. Down the hall, Darren Evans was delivering pizza to Ms. Vera. He took one look at Ms. Vera and knew that he dare not step foot over the threshold. He heard the loud knock at the end of the hall. He saw a beautiful black queen with long thick hair and eyes that looked right into his soul open the door for Esther. They locked eyes. He knew that he must meet her. He knew that he loved her.

Darren came back during the day when he knew Esther was downstairs in the store. He took a deep breath and knocked on the door twice. There was no answer. He waited a few seconds before knocking again. He was sure that he heard noise coming from inside. He thought back to the prior evening and tried the secret rhythm Esther had used. His beautiful black queen opened the door. She was startled and immediately began to shut the door. He placed his foot in the door. "Don't be afraid," he said through the crack in the door. "I'm not here to hurt you. I just had to meet you."

"Who are you?" she demanded to know.

"Look, give me five minutes inside to explain." The door didn't budge. "I know that Esther is downstairs. Look, I don't want no trouble. I just want five minutes of your time, honestly." The door opened and he walked in.

Once inside and up close, he realized Erica was more beautiful than what he had seen of her from a distance. He was rendered speechless. She stood directly in front of him with her arms folded. "Your five minutes is almost up," she said pointing to the clock on the wall. Her voice was like music to his ears.

"Yeah right, look my name is Darren and I saw you the other night when I was delivering pizza down the hall. I just had to meet the most beautiful girl in the world."

She laughed and the room lit up. Darren knew at that moment that he had just entered heaven and he didn't want to ever leave. "I know that my time is up but can I come and see you again sometime?" he asked.

"Well," she blushed and put her finger on her chin as if she were thinking about it. "Sure, I would like that." Darren walked out of the door feeling like he was on top of the world.

For days, weeks and months, Darren came to visit Erica during the day while Esther was downstairs minding the store. Darren told Erica that one day she would be his wife. He told her all about his family and shared his hopes and dreams of their future together.

One evening, Darren left in haste. They had both lost track of the time. Esther would be coming up the back hallway any second. A few minutes later, she came up the back stairs as normal and knocked on the door with the secret rhythm. Erica opened the door. Esther walked into the living room. She stopped in her tracks when she saw the jacket lying across the chair. She spun around quickly to face Erica.

"Where is he?" she demanded.

Erica raised her eyebrows. "Who, Mommy?"

"Don't play with me, chile. Where is he?" she said louder. Erica remained silent.

Darren used the secret rhythm and was smiling from ear to ear when Erica opened the door, the next day. She appeared stiff and looked like she had been crying. Darren walked inside "What's wrong?" he asked. Esther came from behind Erica.

"How dare you try to make fool out of me. You shall pay for what you have done to me." She proceeded to take off her sunglasses. She looked at Darren directly in the eyes. He screamed and dropped to his knees holding his eyes. "You have held your eyes steadfast on my beautiful chile. From dis day forward, you shall never see anything ever again."

Erica cried and rushed to help him.

"Get away from him." Esther pulled Erica away.

"No!" cried Erica. "I love him."

Esther pushed Darren out of the door and slammed it shut.

"Don't you dare tell me what to do and what not to do ever," Esther said. "I raised you and dis is the tanks that I get." She raised her voice. "You are no better than your muda and fada. You are nothing but a liar."

"What did you just say?" Erica turned to face Esther looking very confused. "My parents? You never told me that you were not my mother. How could you?" She turned away.

"Gal, I raised you din't' I? Then dat makes me ya muda."

"No, that makes you the liar." Erica said in disgust.

"Enough!" Esther spat as she spun Erica around and stared directly into her eyes. Erica's crying eyes were filled with innocence and love. The more Esther's eyes penetrated Erica's soul, the more innocence and love they found. There were no weaknesses, and no pain in her soul. There was only purity. Finally, Esther looked away defeated. She sat down in the nearest chair tired.

"You always told me not to trust anyone who lied, cheated or stole from you." Erica stood firm, looked down at Esther and with tear filled eyes and a shaky voice, she said "Well, I must leave this house now that I know that I can't trust you." Erica walked to the door and glanced back only once. She walked out with nothing but the clothes on her back. After the door closed, Esther sat in that chair and cried to herself. She realized that she had let the best thing in her life, the one good thing walk right out of the door.

Erica stepped outside. Darren was nowhere to be found. She went down the back hallway stairs and out the back door still no Darren. She ran around to the front of the House of Meditation. There he was sitting against the building with his head down in his knees. She rushed towards him. She bent down and wrapped her arms around him. "Oh Darren," she cried. "I love you," she said as she held his face in her hands and continued to cry.

Slowly, he wiped her tears away. He began to make out her face. As her tears touched his eyes, he could see clearly. Darren took Erica away from the House of Meditation never to return.

Esther went back to sitting behind the counter daily hoping deep down inside that one day Erica would return to her. That is until, one day a young girl walked up to the counter as Esther was bending down to put something away. When Esther stood she saw that the young girl was pregnant. "What is it dat you seek from dis place?"

The Nubian Princess Tale

The bride lifted her arms in the air and the bouquet came floating in the air towards us. I rushed forward with my arms raised high in the air. The bouquet was coming my way. I leaned into a sea of arms and felt the stem graze my hands. I grabbed with all my strength. I felt a tug but kept my grip until I felt no tug at all. I raised my prize victorious. "Girl, this couldn't be better timing since I'm engaged," I told Gloria my old college roommate, the bride. She and I hadn't seen each other in years even though we now lived in the same city.

"You're kidding!" she said. "I guess your wedding is truly meant to happen. Where's the lucky man?" She started looking around the room.

"He's in Chicago on business."

"Well, when he gets back in town, I want you to come over so I can meet him."

"I'd like that and then we can catch up on what's been going on."

"Yes girl, we have to do the gossip thing. Too much time has passed. We need to get back on track."

"Gloria, we need you. It's time to throw the garter," the wedding planner told her and she proceeded to the center of the room.

I watched as old and young men gathered on the floor to catch the garter. 1-2-3. A sea of men moved in for the catch and then there was some scrambling on the floor. The ring bearer waved his prize in the air. The wedding planner waved for me to come to the center of the room.

"We would like to get a picture of the lucky young man and you." She smiled.

"Aren't you the lucky one getting a younger man," Gloria said from behind me. I turned to her and laughed.

When I turned back to the photographer, the ring bearer was nowhere in sight. "Hi, I'm Keith." He held out his hand and looked at my mouth as if he read lips for a living.

"Wanda," I mentioned nervously. His looks caught me off guard for a moment.

"I bought the garter from little man. I told him that if he caught it and gave it to me that I'd give him $20."

"Are you getting married soon?"

"No, actually it's a tradition for me. Ever since I went to my first wedding and I caught that garter. I've collected them at other weddings as a lucky charm to guarantee that I stay single. I'll stop this ritual when I'm ready to settle." Keith had brown skin, was tall, slightly bow-legged and you could see the muscles through the outline of his suit jacket. He was down right fine.

I looked him in the eye. We were the perfect complement to each other. I am tall, light skinned with an hourglass shape. We were the perfect picture of masculine and feminine.

"Excuse me, look this way." The photographer broke my concentration. Keith grabbed my waist as I placed my hand on his stomach.

"If I didn't know any better I'd think you two were a couple," the wedding planner smiled. "Keith, you'd better not let this one slip through your fingers" she pointed her finger in his direction.

The D.J. started playing Tom Browne's Jamaica Funk. "Shorty, that's our que. What do you say?" He tilted his head towards me.

"Let's do this." I grabbed his hand and strutted onto the dance floor.

This was my song. I started dancing as if I was in my own world with my eyes closed and my back to him, putting my hands in the air, shaking my hips. I felt his hands on my waist and I felt his hips pressed up against my behind. We were jamming. I was so glad that I had decided to come to Gloria's wedding. I was having so much fun. During the next song, a slow jam, he asked, "How do you know Gloria and Cecil?"

"Gloria was one of my college roommates."

"So you and some girlfriends came to the wedding."

"No, I'm solo but I've seen some friends here tonight. What about you?"

"Cecil is my cousin." I nodded. We had an audience during the next song. I was backing that thing up and he was letting everyone know that he knew what to do with it. People started cheering us on and we ended up bowing to the crowd at the end of the record. The audience wanted more but I was hot and my feet were killing me. I shook my head, no more. He took my arm and led me away from the reception to the hotel balcony.

The balcony opened up to a picture perfect view of the Washington D.C. skyline. You could see from the lighted Capital rotunda, past the Washington Monument to Crystal City in the distance. It was a beautiful summer night. There was a nice breeze stirring and the sounds of the city all around us. We could hear a car horn blowing in the distance, a city bus driving by and love ballads coming from the ballroom inside where the wedding was being held. I gripped the balcony rail enjoying the view. I turned around to find Keith taking me in. I kicked my shoes off and held my arm out as I heard the next song beginning from the ballroom. We began to slow dance to Jeffrey Osbourne's "Concentrate on You." He spun me around and I swung my head and shoulder back at the end of the spin.

"Watch out Fred and Ginger." We looked over to see Gloria peeking her head out of the door and we laughed. "Don't let me interrupt. I'm on my way to change and I figured that I'd check out the place. It's beautiful isn't it?" she walked out and peeked over the balcony. She waved as she tipped back inside.

We continued to dance awhile and then we rested on a chaise lounge made for two as we looked out at the city. My mind flashed to Derrick. If he were in town, I wouldn't be at this wedding. He wouldn't have wanted to come and that would have meant that I wouldn't have come either. Even though he would have said that I could go. I need to get out more. I'm so glad that I have this time to myself.

"What do you do for a living?" I rested my head against my elbow laying on the back of the lounge and curled my legs up under myself.

"I'm a telephone technician for the phone company."

"Oh so you're one of those macho guys who walks around bare chested in public flexing your muscles, holding up traffic while the rest of us are trying to go places." He laughed.

"Oh let me guess what you do for a living. You're one of those psychic connection counselors." I shoved him and bent over and grabbed my shoe and acted as if I would hit him.

"Hey" he shielded his face with his arms. "There's no need for violence. Let me clear up some perceptions that I've just heard. I don't bare my chest in public. I'm a very private person." He placed his hand on his heart. "I'm not like other guys." He did his Michael Jackson impersonation.

I laughed. "You're so sensitive."

"No, really I take my shirt off if it's a real hot day and I'm working in the shade but I keep it on if I'm in the sun. I don't need a tan and I definitely don't want skin cancer. So is the psychic connection your full time or part time job at the moment?"

"Well you see I counsel in my spare time." I laughed. "Seriously, being a social worker for the District is my full time profession."

"That sounds like a tough job."

"Oh, believe me, I have my days."

"You know, I'm in the big brother program. My little brother is 8 years old. He has only seen pictures of his parents. He's never met them. It's probably for the best. They were both addicts. So I can only imagine the horror stories that you've seen."

"He's a lucky kid to have someone like you there for him. There are so many boys that don't have role models." He looked into my eyes and kissed me.

A loud bang from the street below broke our concentration. "What the hell?" Keith said as we jumped up. A manhole cover was flying up in the air like a Frisbee. He grabbed my arm and pulled me back.

"You know I've heard about covers blowing off but this is the first time that I've seen it happen," I said to him.

"Well, let's hope this is your last because that can be dangerous." We snuggled back on the lounge listening to the commotion below and the music coming from the ballroom. Before I knew it a couple of hours had passed by. We were both more than a little tipsy from a few Long Island iced teas and too playful. "Can I take you home?" he asked.

We headed to my house in his Lexus. What was I doing? I thought to myself sitting next to him that I should have taken a cab home. I can't sleep with Keith. I won't cheat on Derrick. Even if he comes inside, we'll just talk and that's all, I said to myself. "Oh, I'm sorry Keith. I meant to tell you to take a right turn at the street we just passed."

"No problem."

As we pulled up to my front door, I did the polite thing "Do you want to come in?" He looked at me with a hungry look in his eye. I can handle this with no problem. I said to myself as I got out of the car.

Once inside, I told him to have a seat in my living room that I would be right back. I raced to the bedroom. My head was light from the liquor and I had to pee. Who was I fooling? I wanted a piece of that fine specimen sitting in my living room. Derrick is gone for a month. He won't know a thing besides we're not married yet. As I flushed the toilet and opened the bathroom door, there he was standing outside of the door in my bedroom. He grabbed me and kissed me sliding his tongue toward the back of my throat. I grabbed the back of his head and returned the invitation. He grabbed my behind as I grinded into his hips. I pushed him backwards ever so slowly onto the bed. I was on his lap. I proceeded to unbutton his shirt and kiss his nipples. The bulge in his pants told me that he was ready. I got up and unbuckled his pants and removed them. He pulled up and proceeded to fondle my breast. My body was on fire. He unzipped my dress and removed it. I pushed him back down, sat on his lap and proceeded to ride him as he sucked one of my breasts and fondled the other. I felt as if I was in a drunken lust haze. He pumped my body and I squeezed harder until I felt the sensation rising in my body. I looked at his face and I could feel his pressure level rising to match mine and finally we both shuddered in content simultaneously. I rolled off of him and lay down on my bed happy and exhausted. Derrick had never made me feel this way. That's when I passed out.

I woke up the next morning to the smell of bacon coming from my kitchen. My head felt as if someone had been using it as a drum and the light that hit my eyes was definitely too bright.

"Mornin' sunshine." I peeked from under the sheet to see Keith sitting on the edge of the bed pushing a cup of coffee under my nose. "Drink this."

I moaned as I forced myself to sit up in the bed. "Can you tell the band next door to stop playing so loud?"

"Drink this and the loud music will start to fade after a few sips." As I drank the coffee I got a better look at Keith as he got dressed. He had broad shoulders, well-defined abs, not only was he fine but he was built.

"Well, sunshine, I'm sorry that I have to run but I'm supposed to take Gloria and Cecil to the airport this morning. Breakfast is on the stove. I'll call you," were the last words he said before he tilted my chin, looked me in the eyes, kissed me on the lips and walked out the door.

I looked at the clock. It was 7:30 am. I dozed off and had a dream. In my dream, I was dressed in a beautiful long gown and I was standing alone in a field of flowers. A man was calling my name in the distance. He was coming towards me on a horse. I couldn't make out his face in the distance. The closer he came I noticed his muscular physique. As he came closer, I got excited. BEEP BEEP. I opened my eyes and turned off the alarm clock. It was 9:00. I had to get up and start getting ready for church. This had become another one of my rituals in Derrick's absence.

By mid week, I found myself meeting Keith for dinner. He loved soul food so we met at a soul food joint after work. Afterwards, he took me to his place. The phone rang as he placed the key in the door. "You know that you'd better get your girlfriend's call. Don't mind me, I understand." He rushed to the phone.

"Hello, hold on a minute, I want you to say hi to my friend." He handed me the phone. I looked at him like he was crazy. He smiled "Go on and say hi."

"Hello."

"Hi" I heard a little boy's voice on the phone.

"What's your name?"

"Taj."

"Hi Todd"

"Noo T-A-J"

"Oh, I'm sorry, Taj." Keith had disappeared. I walked around his living room looking around.

"That's O.K. What's your name?"

"I'm Wanda."

"Oh, Keith told me about you." Now the kid really had my attention.

"Did he? What did he say?"

"You're his new friend. He met you at Cecil's wedding." I wanted to ask the kid if Keith told him about all of his new friends but Keith walked back in the room and put his mouth to the receiver.

"Taj, what you trying to do make a move on my woman?" Taj laughed in the phone as Keith took the phone from my hand.

I walked around while he questioned Taj about his day. He had nice African art pieces. Clean kitchen. He must never eat here, I thought to myself. He had a candle burning and two drinks sitting on the patio.

"Come on, it's unwind time." He grabbed my hand and led me out onto the patio. We talked until late and I ended up spending the night. That night, I dreamt that I was dressed in the long gown standing in the field of flowers and the man riding the horse called my name in the distance. I opened my eyes. Keith was saying my name telling me that I had to get up. He drove me home around 5 a.m. so that I could get ready for work. The following week, I met Taj when the three of us went to the Children's Museum in Baltimore. We made dinner at Keith's place afterwards.

As the weeks went by, I found myself lying to Keith and canceling some of our dates because I knew that a relationship with him just wasn't possible. I started telling him that I had a lot of overtime to do at work. However when I felt the need for conversation or company, I made myself available. I began to think about the relationship that I had with Derrick. I began to wonder if I was marrying the right guy. Derrick and I never went to clubs. Not that I'm a club person but being with Keith reminded me of my college days and how much I liked to dance and be around children. Derrick didn't want children for a while - as a matter of fact, he wasn't sure that he wanted children at all, which had been fine with me at the time. I saw enough of them at work. But now that I'd spent time with Taj, I enjoyed having a child around the house. I spent time painting, which is something that Derrick always criticized. He always hinted around that my painting was a waste of time and money. I found that it helped me unwind after a hectic day or week.

Keith began to sense a change in my attitude. He questioned me about it. I told him that things were going a little too fast that's all. He accepted my answer. That's when I realized that I had some strong feelings for the brother. But I chose to ignore them. Derrick on the other hand didn't appear to notice that I was distant during our phone conversations. If he did, he didn't say it out loud.

"Hi, I'm so glad you could come." Gloria greeted me at the front door of her new home. "This must be the lucky man." She held out her hand to Derrick. "Nice to meet you." Derrick nodded as he followed me in the door. "We were just getting ready to set up the VCR to watch the wedding video."

"Wanda, we can't stay. I've made dinner plans for us," Derrick said out of Gloria's earshot.

"Just let me see a few people and the video," I whispered. Gloria showed us the food while we could hear voices of others coming from the family room. Once downstairs, I scanned the faces in the room, some faces were familiar from the wedding. I knew that Keith was at work so as expected he was nowhere in sight. The video was starting. Comments and jokes were made through out the video and then came my five minutes of fame catching the bouquet and there was Keith.

My heart stopped briefly as I realized Derrick was sitting next to me and the wedding planner was on the video saying, "If I didn't know any better, I'd think you two were a couple. Don't let this one slip way."

Then my dance fever debut. I heard Gloria's voice. "Girl, shake that thing. I need you to show me how to do that for Cecil. Ain't that right, Cecil?" Chuckles rang through out the room. Cecil's eyes lit up as he shook his head in approval. I turned to Derrick and the look on his face told me that he was pissed. I got up and found the bathroom. I knew what I needed to do. I thought I'd have more time since this was my first time seeing Derrick in a month. I had him pick me up from work and bring me here. I hadn't even mentioned that it was a get together. Otherwise, he wouldn't have come with me. I was glad that Gloria had invited us since I really didn't want to be alone with Derrick right now.

Just as the video ended, Keith came down the stairs. I immediately nudged Derrick. "Are you ready to go?" He was fuming. I got up and there Keith was standing in front of me.

"Well hello sunshine." He smiled and hugged me.

"Hi Keith" I smiled back. I want to introduce you to Derrick.

Keith held out his hand. "What's up man?" Derrick didn't budge; he just nodded looking Keith up and down.

Just then Gloria came over "You guys can't be leaving, you just got here."

"Yeah, sorry to eat and run," I chimed in.

Gloria searched our faces. "Well, Wanda it was nice meeting your fiancé."

I watched Keith's eyebrows go up.

"So how long have you been fucking Keith?" Derrick slammed his car door shut.

"Excuse me?"

"You heard me, Wanda. Don't play your fucking games with me. You were dancing with that nigga like a ho."

"What? We were just having fun."

"I'm engaged to marry a ho, who thinks that I'm stupid!"

"Derrick, that's why I can't take you nowhere and who you think you calling a ho? You always get the wrong idea about stuff."

"Wanda, you don't dance with some guy like you did on that video and not sleep with him."

"Derrick, how would you know when you don't even dance? As a matter of fact, you don't do anything except work."

"I don't need to dance to know that you fucked that guy. It was written all over both of your faces."

"What are you talking about?"

"Look bitch, I'm not fucking stupid."

"Bitch? Let me out of here right now." He ignored me. I yelled louder "Let me out of the car!"

"You better be glad that I'm giving you a ride." Just then he had to stop for a traffic light. I opened the door and got out.

"Wanda!" I heard him yell as I rushed down the sidewalk.

"Wanda!" I wanted to run back to the car but I couldn't. I was in the dark, surrounded by abandoned buildings. There was a heavy gas odor in the air and trash lined the sidewalk.

A bum sitting on the stoop of one of the buildings yelled "Wanda, don't run baby, come here I'll protect you." I ran over to the parked cars along the street and began walking in the street. I turned to face the traffic looking for a bus or cab.

I could see Derrick slowly following along beside me in his car. There was a car horn. Someone was rushing him to move along. He pulled up ahead of me into a parking space. I looked behind me into the oncoming traffic. I saw a cab. "Taxi!" The cab driver saw me. I got in. As we rode past Derrick's car, I saw that he had gotten out of the car to come and get me. I glanced over at him standing by the car. He was looking at me like I was crazy.

I kept busy the following week at work. I felt like I was coming down with a stomach bug but being the superwoman that I am, I chose to ignore the symptoms. I kept right on going as if I was healthy.

All week I had gotten phone messages from Derrick but I was too sick to be bothered with him at the moment. It wasn't Derrick that concerned me. It was Keith. One night, I dreamt I was standing in the field of flowers and the man on the horse called my name. I got excited and I could see his beautiful smiling face. It was Keith. He stopped his horse in front of me and reached down for my hand. He helped me get on his horse and he handed me a red rose and said, "For a beautiful Nubian princess."

We kissed and rode off into the sunset. I woke up and I knew that I needed to talk to him. I missed him. I finally gathered enough courage to give him a call.

"Hello."

"Hi Keith. It's Wanda."

Dead silence.

"Keith, listen I'm sorry. I'm really sorry that I didn't tell you about Derrick. Honestly, you caught me by surprise from the moment that I first met you. I didn't want to lose you, that's why I didn't tell you about him."

"Yeah, yeah, look, what do you want."

"Friends." I mumbled softly. "I want us to be friends."

"What about Derrick?"

"What about Derrick?" I said loud.

Then he got louder "That nigga didn't look like he wanted you to be my friend when I met him. Listen, I don't need no nigga looking for me out in the streets ready to shoot me cause I'm friends with his woman." I laughed at the thought. Derrick did not fit the physical description of a killer and Keith knew this.

"Look I can be friends with anyone that I want to have as my friend. If Derrick has a problem with my friends then he needs to deal with me directly." I started to feel nauseous.

"O.K. time will tell who the boss really is, " he said.

I breathed heavy and said, "Friends?"

"Uh huh, as long as I don't feel any bullets grazing past my ear."

"Good, can you bring me some soup and ginger ale? I'm sick."

Keith brought me food and he took my temperature and gave me a body massage since my body was aching. He refused to touch my hands and he brought rubber gloves and a face mask because he didn't want to catch what I had since he hadn't thrown up since he was 12 years old.

My period was late - at least I thought it was. I was home sick from work and my stomach was still feeling queasy. I was laying in the bed listening to Oprah and the show was actually making some good points that I needed to hear about relationships. The speaker was talking about how women are the nurturers in a relationship and that role causes them to take care of others, which can take away from caring for themselves if they are not careful. Boy that sounds familiar. I had supported Derrick with his job one hundred percent. If we had a date and he had to work late, forget the date. On the other hand, if I had to work late and we had plans, he became annoyed. He would say you need to quit, you don't like that job anyway or can't someone else in the office do that, why does it have to be you? I got up and found a pregnancy test under the sink. As I waited for the results, I thought about how happy I have been this past month doing things that I wanted to do when I wanted to do them with no questions asked. I wanted to keep doing the things that I liked to do. I looked at the stick. I was pregnant.

I called Derrick and invited him over. As soon as he got in the door, I got straight to the point. "I've been doing a lot of thinking and I think that we need to put the engagement on hold right now." I could tell by the look on his face that he hadn't expected to hear that.

He immediately became defensive. "Wanda, what's going on? I come back to find you lap dancing with some guy and not returning any of my calls. You're sleeping with him, aren't you?"

"Derrick, I'm not going down that road with you today. I need some time to think about how I want to spend the rest of my life."

"Didn't you have enough time to think about all this while I was away?" He was aggravating me.

"Didn't you ever wonder if we were making the right decision?"

He looked me dead in the eyes and said "Not until now. But that's cool. So let me make sure that I got this thing straight. You want to break off our engagement to figure out if you want to sleep with some other dude for the rest of your life or if you want to sleep with me the rest of your life?"

I breathed out loud, "I want to break off the engagement so that I can figure out what I want to do personally for the rest of my life minus any man. Me." I patted my chest. "What I want period."

He just nodded and said. "I guess it's better to find out now than find out in divorce court."

"Derrick, while you were gone I did a lot of thinking and I did a lot of living…my way. I did things that I wouldn't normally do when you're around because you would have belittled what I was doing or you wouldn't have wanted to do those things and I would have wanted to do them as a couple so I wouldn't have done them at all. Well, I did those things alone while you were gone and it felt good. I felt like a new person. I realized that life is too short to live it for someone else."

Keith brought tickets for us to go see Patti LaBelle. I had never gone to see Patti live and he insisted that you hadn't lived life until you saw Patti perform live. I wasn't prepared for the emotions that Patti's songs would take me through. I started crying when she sang Somebody Loves You. Keith had brought a dozen roses with him and we stood with most of the audience waiting to give her our gifts. By the end of the show, I was a Patti fan for life.

On the way home, I told him about my dilemma. He held my hands and looked into my eyes, "So have you reached a decision yet? I'm not rushing you. I'm just trying to get an idea of where your head is at."

"Well, I'm thinking about me and what I want for my life. I have some issues where I have allowed certain things to happen to me. I need to work through those things."

"Are you sure that you can work those out alone?" His question surprised me. He saw pieces of me that I didn't even realize anyone paid attention.

"I don't know."

"Its okay if you aren't superwoman all of the time. Remember you're human. If you need some help, don't be afraid. Ask for the help that you need. What about the baby? If you're not keeping it, you can't take forever to figure out what you want to do. It won't be healthy for you if you wait too long."

"I know."

"Okay. I'm here if you need me."

Derrick didn't have much to say to me these days, which was fine with me, because I didn't have anything to say to him as well. He came and got his things from my apartment.

"So where's your boyfriend?"

"Derrick, get out. Just get your shit and go."

"I guess he'll be moving in next week."

"Bye." I pushed him towards the door.

"Oh I forgot, you've sworn off of men until you find yourself." I slammed the door shut.

Now that I was alone, I picked right back up where I left off before Derrick came back into town. I spent quality time focusing on me. It was pretty tough in the beginning because it was easy to find excuses to do other things around my house like painting or cleaning or doing things for others rather than focusing on my problems. I began reading a daily devotional to start off my day. This made me think about a different piece of my life everyday. I started taking walks around the park using that time to focus on my issues and praying for answers. At night, I used aromatherapy to open my thoughts. I started a journal to record my thoughts and actions for that day or issues that I was trying to sort through in my mind. As time passed, I began to feel an inner peace come over me. I began to see some answers clearly. I knew that I was going to be just fine with me.

I would find myself calling Keith sometimes and when he would bring the conversation around to me he would ask so "Where's your head at today?" If he didn't like my answer, he'd say, "Well I think you need to focus on that a little more. I'll call you later."

I had lunch with Gloria. I was in for a surprise. She was pregnant and really showing which she told me was one of the reasons they had rushed to get married. I shared my story with her. "So what are you going to do?" She had a worried look on her face.

"Derrick is history. You know that sometimes things happen to you to teach you a lesson. Well, I learned my lesson. When it's your life, don't let anyone else manipulate it, do what you think is right. I was losing my identity with Derrick and we weren't even married." I shook my head. "I was doing things to please him. I'm gonna try to go forward in life looking for those signs and acknowledge them when they happen. The baby, I'm having it." I smiled that was the first time that I'd said that out loud and it felt right.

"Regardless of how messed up the situation may be and who the father may be it's not this baby's fault. It's my responsibility to have this child."

Gloria placed her hand on top of mine. "I'm here for you. If there is anything that you need, please don't hesitate to ask. What about Keith? You told me about Derrick but what about him."

"We're friends right now but with the road that I'm on right now, I'm nowhere near ready for another relationship right now. I'm still trying to undo the damage from this last one."

"So where's your head at today?" Keith asked. "I'm going to have this baby regardless of who the daddy is."

"Are you sure?"

"I love this baby regardless of the circumstances that brought him or her here. I am having it."

"What about the daddy?"

I paused a second. "I want to know if you would take a blood test?" I asked. "I've only been with two people in the past two months. I really don't need any added drama right now. If I know the results of your test, then I'll know how to proceed." My heart beat quickly awaiting his answer.

"No problem."

The night before knowing the results of the blood test, Keith and I took Taj "trick or treating" in my neighborhood. Taj was dressed as Simba from the Lion King. "Tomorrow's the big day." Keith looked down at me while Taj headed up a walkway.

"I know."

"If the results are positive, I will be in my child's life."

"From you, I wouldn't expect any thing different."

"I just wanted to say this out loud so that you are aware that I will be playing a role in your life. Regardless of what happens, don't try to act like superwoman. If you need anything, just say so."

I dreamt that Keith and I rode off into the sunset again. I woke up from the dream, sweating and my heart was beating fast. I realized that I had fallen in love with this man. I tossed and turned the rest of the night, what would I do if Keith weren't in my life anymore? Would he feel different if this were Derrick's baby? I called him when I got up that morning. He had left for work already so I left him a message. He told me that he would call when he got the results. At work, I just went through the motions. My mind was a million miles away. All day, I didn't hear from Keith. I checked my machine at home and there were no messages. As I rode the Metro home that evening, I felt a calm come over me. I knew that everything would be alright. Besides, I was going to have my first child. I had a lot to be excited about these days.

When I got home, there was a big box by the door. I brought the box inside and shut the door. When I opened the envelope on the box, the note said "To my baby's mama." Inside of the box was a teddy bear and on one of the bear's legs was the garter from Gloria's wedding with a diamond ring tied to it. Just then the doorbell rang. I opened the door and rushed right into his arms. "Yes!"

Winston's Tale

"Ms. Sadie, is he dead?" Glady's Rodgers stood back from the body that lay on the bus stop bench.

"Let me take a look, chile. I've seen plenty of dead people during my lifetime." Ms Sadie continued making her way to the bus stop bench with her walking cane. There lay a body with a blanket completely covering its face so you couldn't really see much.

"I hope those addicts aren't hanging back around here," Gladys frowned.

Ms Sadie poked the body using the bottom of her walking cane. "Hey there, you O.K?"

"Umph" the head slowly lifted from the bench. As the body rose, the features of a man became visible from under the blanket. "Ma'am, I'm sorry that I took up your bench." He began stretching and wiping the drool from the corners of his mouth and sucking the snot back up in his nose. Ms Sadie and Gladys frowned at each other as a result of his actions. He saw them. "I'm sorry. Let me clean this." He proceeded to clean the bench with his wet and filthy blanket. He jumped up to allow them the bench to sit down. "Winston's the name." He held out his hand to Ms. Sadie as Gladys handed her a piece of newspaper.

"Nice to meet you." Ms Sadie ignored his hand and began opening the newspaper and placing it on the bench so she could sit on it.

"Maybe you can help me? I'm looking for 4910."

Ms. Sadie peeked over her glasses. "Why?"

"I heard that there are rooms for rent and I need some place to stay for a spell."

"That's my house. I'm on my way downtown. I'll be back around noon. Let's talk then."

"Yes ma'am. I'll be waiting." He bowed to her as the bus pulled to the curb. Winston sat down on the bench as if that's where he would be until their return.

"You gonna rent him a room, Ms. Sadie?" Gladys asked as they took their seats on the bus.

"If he can pay the rent and don't cause no trouble, I will."

"You're a better woman than me. From the looks of him, I wouldn't waste my time. I'd send him on his way."

When they returned around 1 o'clock, Winston was not sitting on the bench. He was cleaning the trash and weeds out of the yard of the abandoned house at the bus stop corner talking to himself. "Ms Sadie, I don't know. You sure you want to be bothered with him?"

"Chile, I've lived with roomers that were crazier than a bedbug. As long as his money is green and he can pay the rent, I can deal with him. If he gets too crazy, I know how to get rid of him. I got a piece of iron under my bed that will cure whatever ails him." Ms. Sadie yelled for him as she got off of the bus back at her neighborhood stop as he was busy cleaning the abandoned yard at the bus stop corner. He followed her home. She showed him the room and told him the rules of the house. No loud noise, violence, drinking or smoking in the house. The rent was $40 dollars a week. Winston followed her around the house like he was her child listening to her every word and he paid her enough rent to stay for one week. After their business was settled, Winston went back down to the bus stop corner and continued to finish cleaning up the abandoned yard.

The next morning, all of the trash was scattered all over the abandoned yard again. He scratched his head. "Did you do this?" he said out loud. There hadn't been a windstorm the night before so what the heck had happened? He was confused. He felt a tap on his shoulder.

"Hey old man, get off my turf." He turned to face a pug nosed teenage boy trying to look tough.

"Boy, this here is a free country. Ain't no such thing as your turf unless you got a house built here on this corner and unless I'm blind I don't see your house. " He put his hand up over his eyebrows as a visor looking off in the distance.

"Old man, you heard me." The young boy poked his finger in his face. "You'd better get off our property or you'll have to suffer the consequences. Ugh, man you stink." The boy waved his hand in the air.

"Boy, I've lived a lot of years and I've made it just fine so far without dealing with the likes of you. Now you get your behind off to school and watch the way you livin' because you ain't livin right." Just then a car horn blew. The young boy turned around and ran to the expensive looking car.

"Boy, you're about to get a dose of reality." Winston whispered to himself. As Winston was cleaning the lot later that afternoon he heard a police siren slowing down due to the traffic. He glanced over to the see the pug nosed kid from that morning sitting in the back of the car. "Um huh, He messed with the wrong one. I told that boy that he wasn't living right."

Two days later, the lot was trashed yet again. "I hear you. There is another lesson to be taught before I move on." He said out loud to himself.

"Hey old man, you got my brother busted." Winston turned to see a boy who was practically the spitting image of the boy that had approached him two days ago. "My brother told you to leave this lot alone. Now he's in jail because you didn't do what he told you to do."

Winston scratched his head. "Do I look like I work for your brother, son?"

"Look, old man, leave this lot alone."

"Boy, this here is a free country. I don't see your house on this here property so I can clean it if I feel like it. Now leave me be boy."

"Old man, if you're not gone by the time that I come back, there'll be trouble." There was a car horn and the boy turned around and got into the expensive car.

Later that day, Winston heard the paramedic's coming through the traffic he already knew that the boy from that morning was in the back of the ambulance. "I told that boy to leave me be." The next day, Winston saw a younger child watching him work.

He finally walked over to the child. "Do you want to help me?" The boy nodded his head and smiled.

As they worked the boy said, "You know this is my brother's turf. They would never let me step foot on this property before. They told me that I had to be a member of their gang to set foot on their turf."

"What is your name?"

"Kevin"

"Kevin, you are a good boy. You will go far in this world." At the end of the day, Winston walked Kevin home. He lived quite far away in a poor neighborhood. His mother was not home when they got there. Winston bought him something to eat and waited for the boy's mother.

"What has one of my boys done now?" Harriet grumbled at Winston when she saw him sitting in her house.

"Ma'am, you got troubles and I'm not here to bring you more. I'm here to keep one of your boys out of trouble." He had her attention. "Will you allow your youngest son, Kevin to work for me? I'll pay him, pick him up and bring him home at night. He would be my helper."

"Sure Mister." Harriet didn't care what he did just as long as it brought in some money now that her other two bread winners were out of commission.

"Winston, just call me Winston. Here's Kevin's first day's pay. I'll pick him up at 8 o'clock in the morning."

True to his word, Winston was there at 8 o'clock sharp to pick up Kevin. While walking to work Winston said "Son, I got something for you." Winston went in his pocket and pulled out a necklace "This here is a magic charm that I want you to wear. As long as you wear this necklace no harm will come to you."

"It looks just like yours."

"That's right - it's just like mine. This charm has been in my family for years." Later that day, the expensive car pulled up to the curb and sat there for quite some time. Finally, a midget got out of the car and headed over to them.

"Big Mo wants you off his turf."

Winston chuckled. "Please tell Big Mo that this here is a free country. Unless he owns this property I'm not leaving."

The midget's eyes got big. "Please follow me."

Winston turned to Kevin. "Wait here." Big Mo was tall and real skinny.

He was sitting in the back of the car alone. "I want you to get off my turf."

Winston chuckled out loud. "Lawd, what is wrong with you people? The only way that I'm going to leave this property is if you can show me proof that you're the owner."

Big Mo cracked his knuckles as he looked out the window at Kevin. "Listen old man," he said calmly. "A week ago that abandoned house and that lot there was full of my customers and something physically moved them out of there. No one has lived there in years until I found it and now I'm planning on keeping it."

"Mr. Mo, last time I checked I was the owner of this property. I hit some hard times that caused me to be away for a long time but now I'm back. That is my house and my yard and if you or your people step foot on my property from this day forward, mark my words within a minute they will be physically removed from my property."

Big Mo laughed. "You threatening me, old man?"

"I'm just telling you like it is."

"Little Man," Big Mo put the window down and spoke to the midget. "Little Man, go stand in the yard." Kevin was sitting on the porch steps taking it all in. Little Man stood in the yard. A breeze began to stir. Within a matter of seconds, a heavy wind was blowing through the yard. It knocked the midget down and he rolled out of the yard like a bale of hay while Kevin sat on the porch steps untouched. Big Mo snapped his fingers. The driver proceeded to get out of the car and walk up the steps into the yard. As his foot touched the top step, he flew up in the air and landed at the bottom of the steps as if he had slipped on a piece of ice.

Big Mo nodded "Ah, a challenge. You may go." He waved his hand toward Winston. As the day before, Winston walked Kevin home and paid his mother.

The next morning the expensive car was sitting outside of Kevin's house when Winston arrived to pick him up. "Mister, my boy Kevin can't work with you no more. He got a better paying job."

"Ah, is that right? What is he gonna be doing?"

"He's going to be a messenger for Big Mo." She smiled proudly displaying several missing teeth.

Winston just shook his head in shame. "You got a fine boy there. Don't throw him to the streets to be raised by wolves." Big Mo sat on the broken down couch with a toothpick dangling out of his mouth taking this all in.

"Mister, I appreciate what you done for my boy but don't you dare disrespect my house and tell me how to raise him."

"You right ma'am. No disrespect intended. Can I see Kevin before I go?"

"Kevin!"

Winston took Kevin outside. "Do you have your necklace on?" The boy nodded and pulled the necklace out from under his shirt. "Now I want you to promise me that you won't show nobody your necklace today. Agreed?"

"Agreed," Kevin smiled. "I don't think I'll see you again. My mama says I'm going to be a messenger for Big Mo." Kevin sadly looked down at the ground.

Winston grinned. "Don't worry boy I'll see you in the morning. Now git."

"Who is that at my door?" Ms. Sadie wondered as she got up to answer the door. She opened the door to find Little Man, Big Mo and Kevin standing on her porch. "Yes?" she asked suspiciously.

"Morning Ma'am, the name's Big Mo. I understand that you have a tenant by the name of Winston." He nodded to Little Man. He proceeded to grab Ms. Sadie and push her inside into the nearest chair and began taping her mouth. Big Mo and Kevin walked in and shut the door. "Winston owes me some money." Big Mo proceeded to say calmly. "This young man will wait here with you to collect my money. Kevin, page me when he gets home."

As soon as Big Mo left, Kevin removed the tape from Ms. Sadie's mouth. "Sorry Ma'am."

"Ain't you the boy that's been working with Winston?"

"Yes Ma'am" Kevin looked down at his feet.

"Well what are you doing with those heathens?" she fussed.

"My mother told me that I had to work with Big Mo to make money."

Ms. Sadie shook her head. "Go through the back door down the alley and go get Winston."

One half hour later, Kevin paged Big Mo. Big Mo whistled walking up the steps to Ms. Sadie's house. Little Man knocked on the door. No answer. "Aw just kick it in." Little Man did just that. The house was silent. "Ain't no use in hiding, we'll find you." shouted Big Mo. Just then he lost his footing or so he thought because a force slid him out of the door and down the steps. Before he could regain his senses, Little Man was laying on top of him while the front door slammed shut. He pushed Little Man off of him and he rushed back up the steps to the front door. No sooner than he touched the doorknob, his body began to float. He looked down at Little Man staring up at him. "Get me down," he hollered. He kept floating until his jacket was placed through a high tree branch.

Little Man ran down the street. "Big Mo, I q-q-quit," stuttered Little Man. "I got four mouths to feed. I can't be dealing with voodoo." Winston walked out of the front door with Kevin and Ms. Sadie right behind him. Winston looked up and laughed at the sight before his eyes.

"Man, get me down from here," Big Mo yelled kicking his legs that were dangling from the tree.

Winston kept laughing. "Only if you promise not to bother the three of us ever again. You got that?"

"Who me? Aw, you know I was just joking."

"Oh, you're a joker. Is that it?" The branch holding Big Mo began bending towards the ground. You could hear his jacket starting to rip. He started screaming. Winston laughed more as Big Mo started to fall.

"Man, you playing with me or something?" Big Mo asked angrily. Just then the speed of his fall halted to a stop and his body began going across the sky from side to side quickly. "I was joking, Man." Big Mo let out a nervous laugh as he slowly floated to the ground beside his car. He had a big grin on his face as he landed. He patted his body. He looked toward Winston, Ms. Sadie and Kevin.

"You give Kevin a ride home. Mark my words - harm will come your way if you or your crew lay one hand on him." Big Mo got in his car and left the car door open. Kevin looked over at Winston.

"It's o.k. son. He can't hurt you anymore." Kevin headed towards Big Mo's car. "Oh by the way, Kevin I'll pick you up for work in the morning." Winston yelled behind Kevin.

"I thought you said that he was as smart as your other boys." Big Mo hollered at Harriet as she sat in the kitchen chair cowering at his tone and crying. Kevin sat on the couch and watched.

"If you can't do nothing with him then ain't no hope for him," Harriet said. "Boy get out of here. You ain't nothing but a disgrace and another mouth to feed."

There was only one place that Kevin knew to go. He fell asleep on the porch steps. That morning, he awoke to Winston's voice. "Yes Sir, the house does look good after all these years. It sure does. Watch it Willie, ain't no need to get smart. I did as much work as you did cleaning the front yard."

The boy stood up to see Winston cleaning the front windows. "You need some help?" Winston tore him a piece of the rag that he was using. "Who you talking to?" Kevin started wiping the windows.

"I thought you were asleep. We didn't mean to wake you. I'm just talking to my kin folk." In the reflection in the window standing behind Winston, he could see an old man and a younger man. The boy gasped. He turned to look behind

Winston and no one was there. When he glanced back at the window they were still there standing behind Winston.

"Ain't nothing to fret, boy. That's my pa and my brother Willie. They ain't gonna hurt you long as you a good boy."

Winston grinned, "Long as you keep wearing that necklace that's been in my family since slavery, the spirits will make sure that no harm will come to you. Anyone that tries to disrespect you or harm you will get their wrath instead. Now hustle up, we got a lot of work to do to move in here by the end of the week."

Skeletons in the Closet

"Aw Shucks! Let me get my reading glasses out of my bag. Ain't no way that heffa has won a second hand. Elsie take them glasses off and let me try them on," Sadie said winking at Julia. "I bet they got x-ray vision. She probably can see what's in our hand." They all laughed at the notion as Elsie handed Sadie her glasses. "Oh, oh, they don't have x-ray vision but I can tell you this. I can see out of them clearer than mine." Sadie proceeded to look all around the room with Elsie's glasses on. "This is like seeing a whole new world. I'm not kidding you."

"Elsie's been listening to all of the gossip and she's had time to concentrate on her cards. That's how she's winning. Alright Elsie so what's been going on around here?" Julia asked as she began shuffling the deck of cards preparing to deal the next hand.

"Well, now let's see," Elsie started. "I was waiting at the bus stop one day last week and I ran across Vie. He asked me if I had heard what had happened to Esther's daughter. I told him naw. He said Esther's daughter up and left the house for good. She's running after some boy."

Sadie slapped her hand on the table. "I knew something was wrong over there at the House of Meditations. I told Gladys that something didn't seem right. I went over there the other day and the place was closed. You know Esther's place is open all the time. Aw lawd, Erica is gone. I don't know if I'm going over there for a while now. Cause you know that Esther is one person you don't play with. She's liable to mix the wrong powder up for me if her mind ain't right."

"What you get from her?" Julia peeped over her bifocals. "You know I takes a powder mix for my arthritis. I mix a tablespoon with orange juice and I can get around as good as I did when I was young woman. Did Vie say how Esther was?"

"He said that she's not her self. You know Esther. You didn't know how she was before anyhow. Always hiding behind that cap and those glasses. He said she's walking around like she's lost. She's asking questions of folk more than once," Elsie said as she threw a card on the table. "I know I'm not going for a while now. I'll give her some time to get her mind straight. After she's adjusted to the child being gone. Then I'll go back in there."

"Gin Rummy!" Julia spat at the table.

"Y'all know what? I'm keeping my mouth shut. Cause y'all heffa's are robbing me blind. Especially now that I told you I can't see. But look, speaking of the bus stop, guess who is back in town? Did you see how nice Winston fixed up his house at the corner?"

"I thought he looked familiar but I couldn't place him. That was Odell's first husband. What is he doing back in the neighborhood?" Julia asked. "Well even though they moved across town, he still owned that house. He used to drink so much." Sadie frowned. "Odell put him out cause he would get his paycheck and before he could get home he would spend up more than half his check getting drunk. She couldn't take it no more." Julia shook her head.

"He was my roomer for a week," Sadie said.

"Sadie, no you didn't let that man live in your house for a week."

"Why not, he paid me in advance plus you know I don't take no mess. I read him my rules and told him that he had to abide by them or else he was free to go."

"I seen some boy over there," Elsie said.

"Yeah, I think that must be his nephew or something," Sadie said.

"Nice little fellow. He helped me with my groceries the other day." Elsie said.

"Helped you with your groceries? Why didn't little Cindy go to the store with you and help you?" Julia said with her eyebrow arched up. Elsie looked back and forth at Sadie and Julia and put her cards down on the table.

"I wasn't planning on springing this on you today but little Cindy is pregnant."

"What you say?" Sadie put her hand down on the table.

Elsie let out a loud sigh and said, "I been noticing that she's been getting a little chunky but I didn't think nothing much of it. But I made a note to myself to start paying attention to the trash. I wasn't seeing any tampons or pads in the trash. I said, "Cindy, is there any thing that you want to tell me?"

She just giggled and in that young girly voice she said "Like what grandma? I'm doing okay in school and all."

"I said, like you having a baby and trying to hide it from me. She blushed and couldn't look me in the eye. I made a doctor's appointment for her the next day. I went in the back with her. As soon as she got undressed, I saw the evidence."

"You couldn't tell before then?" Julia peeked through her bifocals.

"You know these young chil'rens these days," Elsie replied. "They wear these big clothes and you can't tell if they fat or skinny or what they might be hiding under they clothes. And baby let me assure you that child was hiding it well. When I saw that belly, I knew that we had a baby coming real soon. She's eight months pregnant."

"Aw Lawd, that baby be born within the month." Sadie shook her head. "Elsie what you gon' do?"

"I called Katrina," Elsie said. "That's her child not mine. She ran off to New York to dance. We both knew that New York wasn't no place for a single mother to raise a child plus she didn't know nobody. I told her that I would take Cindy so that she could get a foothold. Lawd knows she'd been through enough with that no good husband that she used to have. But you know what, that was twelve years ago. Katrina is established now. She's got a house on Long Island. That child should have been up there with her a long time ago. But the time was never right. Katrina was off on tour all over the world. Well guess what, her baby is sixteen now and she and her mother need to get acquainted. As soon as the baby's born, she'll be down. When Cindy is able, they're all going to Long Island to live happily ever after."

"Who's the boy?" Julia sighed.

"Some no good street punk by the name of Amani. He's a runner for that thug, Big Mo," Elsie answered with a frown on her face.

"Lawd, get her out of town quick," Julia said as she shook her head.

"That's what I'm fixin' to do. I don't want no up and coming little criminal in my house. I told Cindy just as much." Elsie replied.

"Ugh, I know that you're going to miss her." Sadie said.

Elsie shook her head slowly. "Sure I am. She was such a big help. But I think this is all for the best. She needs time with her mother. Plus I need time for me. I've had that child since she was four years old. I raised my child way before she came along. I need a break. Plus, I'm looking at retiring soon. When I do, I'm going to sell that house and go back down south."

"When we going?" Sadie asked. "I'm ready myself. We can get us a house down there together. Too many things have changed up here. Things ain't like they used to be when we first moved in the neighborhood. Drugs have come through here. Crooks have come through here. Traffic is coming through here and lots of it. It's time for some peace and quiet."

Elsie shook her head in agreement to Sadie's words. "I'd appreciate it if you two didn't go around saying nothing."

"Honey, don't you worry 'bout a thing. We family here. We been playing cards once a month for how long now? I stopped counting after 4 years. It's hard to imagine that we're the only ones still playing together from our old card party days," Julia laughed.

"Shoot chile, we all got a skeleton or two in our closet. Aw sukie now, what you got Sadie?"

Sadie laughed and looked at the ceiling. "Should I lawd? Alright," she breathed a deep breath. "I'm going to tell you something that only a handful of folks know about me. I, like little Cindy, had a baby out of wedlock. I was fourteen years old. My momma and papa had always stressed the importance of getting an education. While they worked in the fields all day, I went to school. That's where I met Skeeter Tinsley. He was sixteen years old and he was smart as a whip and might I add he was a good-looking young man. He and I were the oldest in the class so we did a lot of our schoolwork together. It started innocent. I was shy."

"Naw." Julia shook her head. "Stick to the story now. This is SADIE that we're talking about." Elsie laughed at Julia's comment.

"Gon' Julia, I ain't always been like this. I got this attitude with old age. I used to be shy before I learned to open my mouth. Anyhow, I was shy. His people lived down the road from us. So we would walk to and from school together sometime. It was on one of these times that we were walking from school playing around when he kissed me and ran ahead of me. Well, I ran after him to hit him only when I caught up to him. He ducked my hit and kissed me again. This time the kiss lasted longer. I was beginning to like this kissing. Then he told me that he wanted to show me something."

"He grabbed my hand and pulled me along 'til I was running to keep up with him. We got to this field of wildflowers when he grabbed my schoolbooks and took off running. I took off running after him. Some of the flowers were mighty high. If you close your eyes you can picture a field of violet, pink, white and orange flowers growing wild all over the place. The field of flowers was simply beautiful. Something you dream about. I was so caught up in the beauty that I lost sight of Skeeter. I began to slow down to enjoy the sight before my eyes when I felt a hard yank on my legs. The pull took me off guard and I fell to the ground. There was Skeeter lying on his elbow with his legs stretched out on the ground. 'You see this field of flowers?' Skeeter asked. One day this is where I will raise my family. My daddy is going to buy this land from Mr. Stokes."

"Stokes was one of the red neck farmers from my town," Sadie clarified for Julia and Elsie.

"He got up and said, 'I'm thinking about building the house over here.' It was next to a big old thick tree. He went behind the tree and came back with a bottle of whiskey. 'My daddy keeps this out here cause my momma don't allow him to drink in the house.' He took a swig and handed it to me. I had never had a drink before in my life. I took the bottle, wiped off the top with my dress and took a swig. Skeeter sat down beside me and took another swig. 'I want a house full of children that look just like you.' Line like that, that boy could have bought me right then and there for the rest of my life for a quarter. You know that boy looked me in the eye and this time I took the bottle from him and took a swig. The liquor was making me hot and happy. Next thing I know we kissing and rolling around in the grass. Hands every where. I was just as drunk and happy. That is until he introduced me to his Johnson. Lawd, I felt that pressure and pain and I started hollering and squirming to get loose. I wasn't drunk no more. It's amazing how quickly you come to your senses when pain is involved. He started kissing me to try and drown out my screams. Then I just started crying. I couldn't fight him. He took my silence as me enjoying myself. He whispered in my ear,' That's it, now we can practice how we gon' fill up my house.' After he got off of me, the first thing that I reached for was that bottle. I needed something to make me forget all of the pain that I was feeling. I don't remember the walk home. I just remember Momma seeing me and breaking down crying at the sight of me. I never went back to school after that. Momma didn't want me nowhere near Skeeter Tinsley. She said that he wasn't nothing but an alcoholic like his daddy. She said that he wasn't never gonna amount to nothing. My daddy said that he would talk to Mr. Tinsley 'bout Skeeter. But my momma was adamant. She wanted me to have a better life than everyone in that town. She didn't want me nowhere near them people. So she did what she considered to be the next best thing. She sent me to live with her sister Bernice. Aunt Bernice was a schoolteacher. I was to be her assistant and help her with her class."

"Aunt Bernice was real strict. During the week, we would go to school and in the evenings we would go to church. Aunt Bernice didn't have any kids and she never let me out of her sight. Within two months of living with Aunt Bernice, I found out that I was pregnant with Skeeter's child. I guess he meant it when he said that we needed to get started filling his house up with kids. After that I started showing. I stayed at Aunt Bernice's house and graded papers for her and cooked and kept the house clean. You know nobody had ever told me how to make a baby and nobody damn sure told me how to birth one."

"As soon as the first labor pain hit my body and Elsie, you know what I mean, it felt like somebody was beating my stomach. I hollered the entire time. 24 hours later, I had a beautiful baby girl. I named her Crystal cause when I looked in her eyes they shined like crystal to me. Her eyes sparkled. She came in this world hollering. But as soon as she heard my voice, she hushed right up. She looked just like her daddy. She was simply beautiful. She weighed 8 lbs. 9 oz, that's why I was hollering so. I went to sleep after all the excitement died down. She was lying right next to me. When I woke up she was gone. My Aunt Bernice had given my baby to one of her rich student's parents. Lawd, I cried for days. My momma said it was for the best. I was barely getting fed she said. How were we going to feed another mouth?"

Silent tears rolled down Sadie's eyes and she became silent. Elsie patted her hand as she watched the faraway look in Sadie's eyes. Julia sat on the other side of her wiping the tears rolling down her face. After awhile, Julia asked, "What ever happened to Skeeter?"

"He drank his self to death. He didn't never amount to nothing. He married for a spell but his wife couldn't stand seeing him drunk all the time so she left him. They never had any children. Plus, he never built a house in the field of flowers."

"What about Crystal?" Julia continued.

"I keep saying that I'm going to find her. You know so many people are finding missing loved ones these days. But I keep thinking that she won't want to see me or she'll hate me."

"Sadie, we're your family right?" Julia asked. "You go and find that child and no matter what happens, we're here for you. Ain't that right, Elsie?"

"Uh huh, do it right away. We'll even help you find out what you need to do."

"You heffa's would do that for me?" A smile rolled onto Sadie's face.

"Yes heffa we would do that for you." Elsie grinned. Sadie put her arms around them both.

"Lawd, it sure does make you tired when you dig something up out of your heart that you've covered for years. It's like racism. You know you turn your eyes and ears away from so much mess that after awhile it gets covered up with new problems. Whew! Alright Julia what's your story, gal?" Sadie patted her eyes with the balled up tissues. The cards were strewn all over the table by now long forgotten.

Julia wrung her hands and took a deep breath and smiled. "Similar to Cindy, I went to live with my mother for the first time at age sixteen. My mother was a beautiful woman." Julia grabbed her pocketbook and dug out her wallet and showed them her mother's picture.

"Oh my, she looks like Lena Horne back in the day." Elsie smiled.

"Let me put on these here glasses and see this picture. Uh huh, she is beautiful." Sadie commented.

"Now you can see where I got my looks from," Julia patted the back of her head with her hand.

"Naw, naw, I was getting ready to ask you so what happened to you?" Sadie crossed her arms and smirked. "Must of took after her daddy's side of the family," Sadie pretended to whisper, but loudly to Elsie.

"Stop." Julia nudged her and they all laughed. "Anyway, my momma was a dancer in New York City during the 30's. She met my father dancing at the black club she used to work at. My father's people had money. He was a dentist and you know to be a dentist back in those days, you were smart and you had a little money. As soon as my father laid eyes on my mother he was in love. Problem was, daddy was married and already had a family. He snuck out the back door on his family to be with my mother. He gave her whatever she wanted with the exception of a divorce from his wife to marry her. So my mother did the next best thing that she could think of to keep my father in her life. She got pregnant with me."

"In the meantime," she continued, "Daddy's wife Ethel began to wonder where he was all the time because he damn sure wasn't at his practice. She hired a private investigator to follow daddy around for a few days. When Ethel confronted daddy with the affair, she demanded that he end the affair immediately. Ethel wasn't going to leave him. She loved money too much plus she was real siditty. She didn't want to draw attention to a scandal because that could affect daddy's business and then she wouldn't have any money."

"Well, daddy told her that momma was pregnant. Ethel almost fainted. She was so outdone that she took ill. Daddy didn't want Ethel to die. He loved her in his own way, but momma was beautiful and she could have any man that she wanted and chose him. Since my mother's occupation was at stake due to her condition, daddy paid for all her wants and needs while she was pregnant since she couldn't very well work anyway. He still saw my mother even though Ethel asked him not to. There was one point that Ethel couldn't fathom and that was that he was addicted to my mother. She was the true love of his life. Prior to my birth, my momma and daddy decided to send me to live with my aunt and uncle to be raised. They couldn't have any children and they too had plenty of money. This suited my momma fine because this gave her the freedom to go back to the dancer life, which is what she loved to do so much.

At the tender age of 4 days old, my daddy took me to live with my aunt and uncle. I grew up in a happy home. My uncle was a doctor and my aunt stayed home all day. I didn't want for anything. I had the best of everything, clothing, food and toys. My aunt and uncle told everyone who knew them that they had adopted me through an orphanage. You know back in those days they didn't go around advertising adoption agencies for black kids. Only my daddy, Ethel, my aunt and uncle knew the story. They definitely didn't tell me."

"When I was around 13, my aunt began taking me to teenage socials so that I could mingle with all of the other siditty black kids. There was one boy in particular that I had my eyes on during that time, Reginald Whitaker. He was smart and witty. He had curly locks and he was light skinned. Plus, he paid attention to me. We could talk for hours about each other's friends, family, and music. We could talk to each other with ease. I didn't tell anyone that I liked Reginald because I didn't want to ruin the friendship in any way. I was willing to wait and see if anything just developed on its own."

"Years went by and we remained friendly. One day, his sister invited me to spend the night over her house. We went down in their basement to listen to records. Their parents had a bar set up down there. Unbeknownst to her parents, we would sit down there listening to records getting "drunk as a skunk". Reginald snuck up on us after we had gotten more than a little toasty. He made himself one and joined us. I was sprawled out on the floor. His sister went to the bathroom and he laid down next to me on the floor and he kissed me. My heart was beating fast and all I kept thinking was I got him now. I finally got him. Before his sister came back in the room, he whispered in my ear and asked me to come to his room after everyone was sleep." I whispered back, "Your sister will hear me get up."

"Once she's sleep, she's out cold. She won't hear a thing, I'll come and get you," he replied.

"In the middle of the night, he woke me up and took my hand and led me down the hallway to his room. Sure enough, the entire house was sleeping. He shut his room door and we crawled into his bed. We hugged and kissed and were happy as two clams in one shell. I was sleeping with Reginald Whitaker my idol. I was on top of the world."

"After we had sex, I snuggled up with him under the covers and we fell asleep. I woke up to a tap on the shoulder. Reginald's momma and their maid was standing over Reginald and me laying in his bed naked." Sadie's mouth popped wide open and she put her hand over her mouth and burst out laughing. Elsie pressed her lips together and smiled. "Oh, I see how this works. I sit here and sympathize with you two and you laugh at me," Julia said folding her arms across her chest.

"We're not laughing at you," Elsie says calmly. "We're just laughing at the situation."

"I know. I'm just teasing." Julia smiled.

"A sight it was. Within 30 minutes, my aunt was there to pick me up. She apologized and all I remember Reginald's mother saying is 'get that little tramp out of my sight.' She kept holding her head like she was going to faint or something. Heffa probably never had sex with her husband. Stuffy. Those folks were just stuffy. They were so stuffy that they were fake. Real folk don't act like that. Now you know if you found your child in bed with some girl, you would cuss her out and kick her out."

"When I got home. My uncle was waiting for us."

That's when he dropped the first bomb. "Young lady, go wait in the living room until your father gets here."

"Father?" I said.

"Go now." He pointed to the living room.

I sat in there for probably five hours. As a matter of fact, it was around dinnertime when daddy finally came in the room. I said "Uncle Ted?"

"Have a seat. I want to talk to you."

"You're my father?" He breathed heavy out loud. He told me the bare bones story of my birth. My momma filled in the important details later.

Then he said, "Now I'm here to take you to live with your mother!"

"What?" I couldn't understand what he was saying.

He just kept right on talking. "You can no longer live here. You've disgraced your uncle and aunt amongst their friends. You must leave."

"But what about my friends?" I asked.

"You'll make new ones. Now your things are packed. We must leave."

"I was in tears. In the course of a day, my entire life had been turned inside out. I was sixteen years old. I was being removed from the only family and friends that I'd ever known. I begged. I pleaded. I was pulled through the door and lifted into my daddy's car. By the time we got to my momma's house, I was asleep. I woke up the next morning with sunshine streaming through the window and my beautiful mother sitting on the edge of my bed. When I opened my eyes, there she was smiling at me."

Then she said, "I know it hurts like hell. But baby now it's me and you and I'm here to tell you that's it's gonna be alright."

"She was my best friend from that day until the day she passed away about eighteen years ago. Lawd, I miss her." A tear rolled down Julia's cheek.

"I hope and pray that Katrina will have that same kind of relationship with her Cindy once they live under the same roof," Elsie said.

"They may have a couple of growing pains but they'll probably do just fine. They'll have that baby to keep them in order. Katrina's not gonna see her grandbaby out in the cold," Sadie said.

"Elsie, you just stay put down here for awhile and don't get into those growing pain disagreements that they're going to have. You just tell them that they need to work things out up there. Tell them that they're both younger than you or better yet you've raised your kids already," Julia replied.

Elsie shook her head and she looked relieved. "You're right. You two can help me stay on track. Then I can do some of the things that I want to do for me."

"Now you're talking. So now that we've solved the world's problems, I got a card score to settle at this table." Sadie picked up the cards and began shuffling the deck.

Beware of Red Toenails

"Bing! The captain has turned off the fasten seatbelt sign. You are now free to roam around the cabin of the aircraft." I opened my eyes. I wished that they would stop turning that damn seatbelt sign on and off every 5 minutes and let a brother catch a nap. I was looking forward to this much needed time off. I woke up earlier this morning and met my assistant down at my new store to make sure that he understood that the painters needed to be finished by the time that I got back next week. We walked thru all of the prep set up that he would oversee while I was gone. I'm on this plane as a result of my doctor's threat about putting me on blood pressure pills if I didn't make some lifestyle changes real soon. I'm in the process of opening my fourth independent African American bookstore. I was viewing this vacation as a fun fling. I was tired of chasing women and I knew it. I had made up in my mind that I was ready to settle with one woman when I found her. I wasn't in a rush to find her. I knew that she would appear when the time was perfect. However, I knew for sure that chasing skirts was no longer a part of my resume. Unlike my boy, I looked across the aisle. My boy, Butter was snoring and laying his head on some woman's shoulder. The woman shook her shoulder and his head was jerked straight up and then it bobbed towards the aisle. He had slept through this flurry of activity. Butter's real name is Scott Johnson. He was known for being smooth with the ladies; that's how he earned his nickname back in the day. He's so smooth that when his wife caught him sleeping with another woman, she wasn't even mad. You know most women in that situation take that act as a license to kill on the spot. But not Butter's wife, Nicole; Nicole walked in on him and his girlfriend. Renee saw her first. Renee screamed and beat Butter on the back. He thought that she was screaming out in pleasure until she went hit him hard again and started pushing him off of her. Once he jumped up, that's when Nicole saw that not only had they been getting busy, but a baby was on the way.

Nicole said, "If you wanted to sleep around, you should have said so a long time ago. I would have gladly left." She swung her neck around with much attitude. "Butter, you're just trifling." Her top lip curled into a frown. "You're lazy, unsanitary, stanking feet and all, and you're broke as shit." By this point, Nicole had started wiggling her index finger in their direction. She switched her index finger in mid point over to his girlfriend and said, "Girl, may God bless you. I'm here to tell you, you're about to raise two children not just one." She cocked her head with a smirk on her face and looked over at Butter. Then as she walked away, she looked up at the ceiling and said real loud, "Thank God, we never had any children." Three weeks later, his girlfriend lost the baby and within a month, they were through. When Butter told me that he had gotten caught, I told him that he was lying. When I heard how calmly Nicole seemed to take it, I told him that he probably hadn't been giving Nicole enough for awhile and she probably had a boyfriend on the side herself. But she still let him hit it every now and then stanking feet and all.

"Bing, ladies and gentlemen, the captain has turned the seatbelt sign on. We will be landing in Montego Bay, Jamaica in approximately 20 minutes. The temperature there today is sunny and 85 degrees." I nodded and looked over at my boy. That's what I'm talking about, some warm tropical weather; perfect conditions to meet some fine, fun, vacationing females. Across the aisle, one of the stewardesses was slipping my boy her digits. We hadn't even landed yet and he had pulled a female already.

Once we checked in, we decided to find our rooms and meet up at the hotel bar around 7 p.m. The hotel had a Spanish hacienda look. I was sitting at a table in the bar, drinking a double tangeray bopping to Bob Marley and the Wailers singing *No Woman, No Cry*. I was feeling the tropical atmosphere, when this beautiful woman walked in the bar. A shapely tall drink of water with a flawless milk chocolate complexion, long black hair dressed in a pink camisole and jeans that accentuated her shape. She walked right up to me. "Is your name, Russ?" She smiled and asked in a clipped accent. My eyes went up as I nodded. "Hi, I'm Veronica Watson. My friend, Sandra is with your friend, Scott right now. She called me and asked me to meet her down here at the bar. She told me that you would be waiting for Scott here. Do you mind if I join you?"

"Certainly. Not at all. What can I get you to drink?"

"I'll have a Sex on the Beach." My eyes went up. She laughed at my facial expression.

"The drink."

"Okay, I was just checking." Once her drink order was placed, I asked her, "How did you know who I would be?"

"Sandra told me to look for a handsome gentleman with beautiful long dreads. So if your dreads looked unruly I would have known that you weren't the right person."

"So, you're a dreads expert."

"I was born and raised on this island. Let's just say, I've seen my share of neat and unruly dreads."

"An island native, I'm impressed. I detected an accent when you spoke. I knew you where from some island." A beautiful island native. I was feeling this woman. It was something about her. She took my hand and she turned my palm face up.

"May I read your palm?" I laughed at her suggestion.

"Sure why not. Be sure and tell me when I hit the lotto." She glazed at my palm and she started running her fingertips across a line in my hand.

"You have a very prosperous career." She said very impressed and I shrugged my shoulders.

"If I were richer, I would probably say yes but all in all I can't complain."

"What do you do for a living?" I frowned at the mention of her question.

"Wait a minute, can't you tell by reading my palm?" She giggled as she looked at me. She had beautiful light brown eyes.

"It's not that descript." I nodded.

"Ok my fault. I thought you were pulling a Ms. Cleo move on me for a minute." She laughed again as I glanced at her sideways. "I own three African American bookstores in the Washington D.C. area. Business is booming and I'm opening my fourth store by the end of this year." She was still holding my palm in her hands. "What else can you see?" I asked in an animated Jamaican accent as I nodded in the direction of my palm. She laughed. This woman is gorgeous. I watched as her expression turned serious as she looked back at my hand. Oh shit, I hope she doesn't tell me that I'm dying or something. I took a deep breath.

She rubbed a line in my hand. "Hmm... You will meet your soul mate very soon. That is if you haven't already." I chuckled.

"Whew, I thought you were going to tell me that I was dying or something." Her eyes shot up.

"Oh my God no, you have a very long life ahead of you. I'm sorry." She smiled. "I didn't mean to mislead you but seriously." Her expression takes on a serious appearance again. "Before you end up with your soul mate, you'll meet someone that is up to no good and that could delay developing a relationship with your soul mate."

I laughed.

She looked at me with a serious expression. "Be careful."

"Hey Girl, I'm glad you're here." Our heads turned to Butter and Sandra, the stewardess from our flight walking towards us. Sandra had her luggage with her. Veronica and Sandra hugged. "Girl, I'm glad to see you. I'm ready to go crash at your place." Veronica turned to me and Butter. I introduced her to Butter.

"If you ladies are leaving then we'll walk you out." I followed her out as Sandra and Butter talked and followed us. "If you have time in your schedule before I leave, I would like it if you could show me around."

"I would love too." We exchanged phone numbers and promised to talk the next morning.

"Man, let's hit the streets." Butter said as Veronica drove off. "Sandra told me about this party going on." The party was jumping when we got there. Drinks and hor d'ouvres are flowing. I'd switched to coconut rum and coke. I was walking around checking out the sights. My boy was working on his next catch. He was out on the dancing floor and I was standing against the wall just checking it all out when this light skinned sister came and stood next to me.

"It's hot in here ain't it?" She frowned and fanned herself. I turned and nodded my head. One of her front teeth is gold. "It's too hot to be dancing and stinking up your clothes and messing up your hair? You wanna go outside." I nodded and I followed her out to a back patio that opened out to the ocean. The sky is a navy blue and flood lights from the building are pointing at the water. You can see the angry waves rolling ashore. I gravitated to a pair of empty chairs on the patio and she followed.

"So where are you staying?" She asked. I responded and she said "We're staying at the same hotel." As she smiled, her gold tooth shined as the light hit it. Butter came out and told me that he was leaving with the girl from the dance floor. They were going to another party. "Man, you go ahead. I going to grab something to eat and chill." I yawned as I started to begin to feel the effects of my day.

"You cool." I nodded.

"Do you mind if I join you for dinner? I haven't eaten myself."

"I don't normally eat with someone that I don't know at least their first name." Her eyebrows went up.

"Oh, I'm sorry. I'm Red." She held up her hand. I looked down at her fingernails and toenails. She had red toenail polish and the word Red written in white on each one of her fingernails.

"What's your real name?"

"Regina, but everyone calls me Red."

"Ok, Red, it's nice to meet you. I'm Russ." We shook hands. We decided to head back to the hotel and have dinner in the restaurant. The ambience was dinner by candlelight. Red was a talker. I started feeling the affects of my day hit me even more so I let her do the talking as I relaxed with some wine. At the end of dinner, I felt her feet rubbing my legs under the table. I already knew that it wasn't that kind of party. I ignored her advances. She started running her fingers across her low cut blouse. I remember paying the check and telling her that I was going to crash.

I woke up the next morning to bright sunlight peeking through the patio sheer curtain. I could hear the ocean waves crashing up on shore and I could smell the salt in the air as I felt a warm breeze blow into the room. My patio screen was open. I turned over enjoying the feel to my senses and then I jumped. Red had her head in one arm and she was staring at me half dressed.

"I've been waiting for you to wake up for the past three hours. I tried to wake you, but you were sound asleep. You told me to wake you up at 8 o'clock. She said nonchalantly. "I need to get paid so that I can leave." She continued.

"Paid?" I raised my head up off of the pillow with a frown on my face. I went to bed alone last night. What is she doing here? Was I that drunk?

"Yeah, what did you think last night was free? This was no love connection for me so I sure hope it wasn't for you. Now you can give me my $1000 and I'll be on my way."

"$1,000? Hell no, I'm not giving you anything." I got up and started putting my pants on that were lying on the floor from last night.

"Okay fine, $500 then but that's the lowest I can go or Barrington will kill both of us." She said as she sat on the edge of the bed.

"Barrington?"

"That's my sugar daddy."

"Get out!" I pointed at the door.

"Hell no, I'll call Barrington if I have to get out." She got up and put her pants on. "Hmph, it's your life." She walked out, slamming the door shut as the phone rang.

"Hi there, Russ, it's Veronica, did I catch you at a bad time."

"No, not at all." I can't believe the chick that just left my room.

"Did I wake you? She sensed the hesitation.

"No, I woke up a little while ago."

"Oh ok, you feeling up to some sightseeing today. I'm available to show you around."

"I'd love one of your personal island tours today." She came to pick me up in her topless jeep Cherokee. She was wearing a turquoise string bikini top and some jean shorts and a pair of timbers. After sightseeing all morning, she took me to her place for lunch. Her backyard backed right into the ocean and she set up our lunch so that we were looking at the ocean as our view. As she prepared our meal, I walked around admiring her art pieces. Art decorated her home to the extent that books decorated mine. I have books strategically placed through out my house and I have bookcases lining the walls of my home office. She had drums, lots of straw mats, dolls and wall hangings. The wall coloring of each room in her home gave her home a very warm, tropical vibrant light and airy feel. I felt right at home and I got a better sense for this beautiful woman who I am really enjoying getting to know. She told me during lunch that she used to work with Sandra as a stewardess. That is how they became friends. Sandra stays over when she has flight layovers. She had taken Sandra back to the airport early that morning so that she could prepare for her next flight. Veronica left the airline to start her own business. She loves to paint. She had sold a number of her paintings and she had gotten to the point that she was making more money selling her paintings than working as a stewardess. She was going to show me her studio after lunch. Just then my cell phone rung, it was Butter looking for me. We were supposed to hook up that afternoon. Veronica's studio was in a back room in her house facing the ocean and it was just as warm and vibrant as the rest of the house.

"Why don't you let me paint you?" She asked as I walked around her studio admiring her work.

"Hmm… I've never posed for a painting before. Do I have to sit perfectly still for like 8 hours? Cause, if so, then forget it." I can't sit still for 8 hours when I'm supposed to be relaxing on vacation, so I know I can't do it for a painting." She laughed out loud.

"I'll make it real simple, and no you won't have to sit still for long."

"Well then, you got a deal."

"Great, we'll get started in the morning."

I watched Veronica drive off after she dropped me off at the hotel. My little island honey. I smiled to myself. I turned and there was Red walking towards me saying "There he is!" These two guys grabbed each of my arms. I resisted.

"Get your damn hands off of me!" A car pulled up and stopped in front of me as the tires screeched. The back tinted window went down and I heard a man say "'Pay up the $1,500 that you owe me for Red's services by tomorrow night or else." Red and the two guys got in the car and the car tires screeched as they left.

The doorman came over to me. "Sir is everything alright?" I nodded and walked inside. I couldn't believe this exploitation shit. I went looking for Butter and he wasn't in his room. I left him a message to call when he got in. I thought about going to the cops but here I am dealing with some bogus bullshit in Jamaica. For all I know, they'll lock my ass up for life for something that I never even did. I felt like I was in a third world country. I went for a swim to try to clear my head and I ate a little dinner. I tossed and turned that night and I woke up in the morning feeling like I had the day before. I had just finished getting dressed when the phone rung, Veronica was waiting for me outside. She took me for a beautiful morning ride. We ended up at this beautiful secluded beach.

"You look like you need your strength before we start working." She pulled out a picnic basket and blanket from the floor of the back of her jeep. She could see the dark circles under my eyes. My mind reflected back on my problem. We ate our croissants and fruit on the beach. "Ms. Watson, you are amazing." I smiled at her gorgeous face.

"This is strictly business. This is how I treat all of my clientele."

"Well, I'm here to tell you that you always have to mix a little business with some pleasure." I leaned over and gave her a kiss.

"Not so fast." She said after we stopped for air. "We need to take a little dip in the ocean." She jumped up and stepped out of her jeans to her bikini bottoms and ran towards the ocean. I was right behind her. We played in the ocean for awhile. Finally, we made it back to the blanket to dry off. We kissed, cuddled and my mind drifted back to my problem. "What's wrong?" She asked as she stared at me lying on the blanket. I took a deep breath and I told her the whole story. I stressed that I never slept with Red; never ever. I was drunk, but I was not that drunk. Veronica listened calmly while I finished my story. I figured that she'd dump me but I just needed a sounding board. "Don't worry, I know someone that can help." I stared at her.

"I'm not paying them any money." I stated clearly.

"No you shouldn't have to pay them. Don't worry. Let's finish up our work here first and then I'll take you to see someone that can help you. Don't you trust me?" She grabbed my hand and looked me in the eye. I trust her. I moved towards her and she stood up. "Nope, no more playing. Playtime is over for now. We're here to work. Get up and get your stuff." We packed up and drove to a portion of the same beach that had a large rock on the sand. We got out and she told me to sit on the rock facing away from the ocean. She pulled a camera out of her bag and she started snapping my picture as I move around in various poses. Finally, she said, "Okay, I've gotten all I need to do your painting. Now let's go see my Aunt See."

To get to Aunt See's home, we drove down a long dirt road off of the main road until finally, the long driveway opened up to a home that backed to the ocean similar to Veronica's. "Aunt See!" Veronica yelled as soon as she turned off her Jeep.

"I'm around back, Ronnie!" We walked around the back of the house to a small animal pen made of wire. There was a little old gray haired lady throwing what appeared to be feed into a pen of chickens.

"Auntie, I brought by someone that needs your help." Aunt See turned to face them and there stood an elderly lady with blue eyes.

"Who is this handsome stranger that needs my help", she smiled and held out her hand. Veronica nudged me to take Aunt See's hand. "I don't bite", she continued. "I'm just an old woman that can't see as well as she used to, but I can see well enough to see that you're a good looking fellow." She laughed. "Walk with me to the patio so that we can talk. Ronnie, I made some tea. Go bring some for us to drink and visit for awhile." She held on to my hand and as we walked toward the patio. She pointed out her goats on the side of her house and some of her plants. With the exception of the waves crashing every now and then, it is very picturesque and peaceful. By the time we got to the patio and sat down, she looked at me and said, "Your problem can be solved. That gal and those boys are taking advantage of you." I was shocked. I hadn't even told her my problem and yet she knew what was wrong.

"May I ask you a question?" She nods.

"How do you know about the girl and her friends?" She smiles.

"It's in your hands."

"It is?" I'm amazed.

"Do you like my niece?" she asks me. Veronica has returned with the glasses of tea for each of us.

"Aunt See, may I call you Aunt See?"

"Certainly."

"Aunt See, I like her very much. You knew that already though didn't you." She laughed.

"Ronnie, I see that you've met your soul mate." She smiled.

"Auntie, I have." She smiled at me. Aunt See turned to me.

"Red and those boys prey on tourists seeking large sums of money. You have done nothing to Red. Everything she tells you is a part of her act." Aunt See got up and went into the chicken coop. She returned with a bag containing a brown powder. "Blow this on Red and those boys and they'll go away. They won't bother you anymore. Now you came to the island with a friend, correct?"

"Aunt See, I sure did. Why do you ask?" I was surprised.

"They have your friend. Go and get him before there is trouble."

"Is he okay right now?"

"He's okay right now, but don't wait long. There could be trouble if you do. Hurry Ronnie! Take him back to the hotel. They will be there. Hurry!"

Veronica and I jumped up. "Aunt See, what do I owe you?"

"You will be family soon. Services for family are always free."

As we walked thru the parking lot back at the hotel, the car from the day before pulled along side of them and the back window went down, "You got my money, heh?"

"Yup, I got it. But I hear that you've got my boy. I'll pay you double if you take me to my boy. He'd better be alive or there'll be trouble."

There was a pause and then I heard "Get your car and follow us." We followed the car to a secluded compound that looked vacant. We got out of the Jeep and followed Red, Barrington, and their henchmen through a vacant courtyard to what appeared to be the compound's living room and down a hallway with rooms on either side of the hallway. We began to hear moaning noises as we continued down the hallway. Red opened the last door on the left.

"What is this?" She walked in the room and we all followed. Butter's arms are in chains coming from the ceiling and there are chains around each of his ankles. All he has on are his underwear. There is a girl with a tight blouse and a shirt tied around her waist and cut-off shorts and she is licking his body. Butter is moaning out of pleasure.

"Shana!" one of the henchman yelled at the girl.

"What do you think you're doing?" He sucks his teeth. I take it that Shana is the henchman's woman.

"What do you care, Hector? You leave me here alone and you expect me to just sit here and be bored. I know that you're sleeping with Red behind Barrington's back."

"What!" I hear Barrington's voice boom and Red's skin is taking on the tint of her nickname. They all begin to talk at once and Shana pushes Red and Shana drops what looks like the key to Butter's chains. I get the key and started to unlock Butter while Barrington and his henchmen try to breakup the cat fight. I handed Veronica the powder. Just as I unlocked Butter's last chain, they were all on the floor fighting. Veronica stood at the edge of the bodies on the floor, threw the powder from the bag onto them, and we run out of there. I could hear coughing and choking as we ran down the hall.

By the time we get safely back to the hotel, it was nighttime.

I wake up the next morning to the salt smell of the ocean in my nostrils and the sound of the ocean waves crashing onto shore. The bright sunlight is peeking through my room's curtain. I turned over and there is Veronica staring at me, holding her head in one hand. "Good Morning Sunshine." She gave me a kiss.

"Let's go get some breakfast. I'm starving." I looked over her shoulder and she had painted my portrait. "When did you have time to do that?"

"I'm a professional. I could paint your portrait in my sleep. That took no time at all." I've fallen in love with this woman.

We had breakfast out on the beach. "Now this is just what the doctor ordered." As I look at her and the view, I didn't want her out of my sight. "Will you come home with me while I wrap up a few things with the new store? I would like to spend more time with you." She smiled.

"I would love it."

"Good Morning my people." We turned to see Butter and Shana walking towards us. "Mind if we join you?" Later during breakfast, Shana and Veronica happened to get up and go to the buffet to get more food.

"What is she doing here?" I don't need anymore drama.

Butter shrugged his shoulders. "Man, what can I say? We're made for each other. She came here last night. You know we had to finish what she started. I couldn't leave this island until I saw her again. Now that my curiosity has been satisfied, it's time to catch that flight this afternoon."

When I opened my eyes during our flight home, Veronica was asleep with her head resting on my shoulder. I could hear Butter across the aisle saying, "So can I get your number?" I just smiled to myself and closed my eyes. Some things never change.

Dealing with the Hand You've Been Dealt

Wendy opened her father's bedroom just in time to see Edwina tryin' to stuff her big behind in a girdle that looked two sizes too small. "What the...," Edwina stopped mid sentence, startled when she realized a teenage girl was standing in Joe's bedroom door staring at her. Wendy stood frozen in shock.

"Who are you?" she frowned and said.

"My name is Ms. Russell young lady and your name is?" Wendy ignored her and walked over to her father in bed still asleep. She couldn't believe that her father had brought a strange woman into her mother's bed.

"Daddy", she walked over to her father who was still asleep and shook him. "Daddy."

"Huh?" he raised his head off the pillow.

"Daddy who is this?" she said annoyed as she waved her hand in Edwina's direction like she was a waving a fly away.

"I'll talk to you about it later."

"Daddy, I think we need to talk about it now before I leave to go to my first class," Wendy said as if she were in charge.

"Don't you see someone else in here? If you can't wait until later then leave my room and wait. I'll be with you in a little while," her father responded loudly. Wendy was steaming hot. She slowly left the room and slammed the door shut behind her.

Joe rested on his elbow on his pillow and let out a loud sigh. "Wendy!" he yelled.

She slowly came back to the door. She left the door closed. "Huh!" she said from outside the door.

"Wendy, open the door," he said softly. She slowly opened the door.

"Yes daddy?" she said softly as she peeked her head in the door. "Baby girl, close my door the right way." She smiled at her father and glanced over at Edwina and rolled her eyes. Edwina had managed to wiggle a few more inches into her girdle. Then Wendy pulled the door closed softly. "Thank you, baby," Joe said softly.

"Oops! Daddy looks like your baby girl ain't too pleased to see me here." Edwina turned to face Joe as she made her final wiggle into her girdle.

"She's just not used to finding anyone in this room with me besides her mother, that's all."

"Well, it sounds like now is the perfect time for you to let her know that I'll be moving in." Edwina wiggled her double D cleavage in his face as she struggled to close the button blouse across her chest.

Joe felt a strong ringing in his head coming from the hang over he had been ignoring up until now. "What?" he asked with a frown on his face.

"Wait a minute. I'm not trying to tell you how to raise your daughter. If you don't want to tell her now that's totally up to you. I got enough on my hands letting mine know that we're movin' in here. But you and I can talk about the details tonight at the club."

She glanced at her watch "Look at the time. I gotta get ready to run or I'll be late for work." She bent over and put on her pumps. He rubbed his hand over his face.

"What'd you say about tonight?" She laughed at his reaction.

"You silly sleepy head. I know you're tired after begging me half of the night to move in so that we can be together every night." She smiled proudly. "What really convinced me was the key." She held it up in front of his face. "You told me that this here key was special because it used to belong to your dear deceased wife."

He looked over at the nightstand and there was the key chain with the initial V that held Vivian's keys to the house.

Edwina grabbed the key and a small bottle off of the nightstand and put them both in her pocketbook. What was I drinking last night? He thought to himself as he got up and put his robe on. He couldn't remember a thing. He knew one thing for sure that woman was too much from what he caught a glimpse of this morning - too much make-up, too much perfume and fat. Maybe he was starved for the female touch more than he cared to admit. He shook his head in pity at the thought.

"Baby girl," he hollered as soon as he let Edwina out the front door. There was silence. "I know that you hear me."

"Yes daddy," Wendy hollered from the kitchen.

He sat across from her at the kitchen table where she sat with her nose buried in the newspaper. "Can I talk to you?" She kept reading the paper. He reached his arm across the table and smashed the paper with his hand.

She stared at him with plenty of attitude on her face. "Daddy, how could you sleep with that woman in our house? Ma hasn't been dead 6 months yet," she said with disgust.

He saw the pain in her eyes. "I'm sorry," he said calmly. "I should have formally introduced you both first. We should have spent some time together so that you could get to know one another. I didn't mean for this to happen. Baby, I loved your mother. My God, I still do. This whole thing is my fault. I'll do better next time."

She raised her eyebrow. He caught her look. "That's right, next time. I hope you don't expect me to be a lonely old man the rest of my life?" She paused for a moment and shook her head no.

"Daddy, I understand. I do. It's just to see you with her unexpectedly," She waved her hand.

"Now you may not have seen the last of her," he arched his eyebrows at her. "I may be seeing more of her. So I'll expect you to show some of that respect that your mother and I taught you."

"I'll try." She said in a flat tone.

"That's fair enough. Now give your old man a kiss and get out of here before you're late for your first class."

A few minutes later she yelled downstairs to him, "Daddy where's ma's key? I can't find mine."

He looked up at the ceiling. Of all days, she needed the spare key today. "Uh, look on my dresser and just take mine."

Joe went to work at the club that evening still trying to piece together the events from the night before. The bartender interrupted his thoughts as he sat alone at the bar early that evening. "Bro, what's on your mind?"

"Women," Joe said with disgust.

"Ah, spill it. You know it ain't nothing I can't help you solve. I ain't got the female anatomy but I definitely got the female mentality. Now what can Ms. Vera help you with?" Joe swallowed the rest of his drink.

"V, you know that woman that you introduced me to last night? She's trying to move into my house."

"Damn, I need to talk to her. She knows how to throw something on a brother." V could tell by the look on Joe's face that he wasn't amused. "I'm sorry I got side tracked for a minute. That's kind of quick ain't it? I mean Joe, do you even know if she grinds her teeth in her sleep? Does she have false teeth or wear a wig? Come on work with me." Joe laughed.

"Do you know?" Joe asked and raised his eyebrows.

"She ain't no friend of mine," V quickly answered. "She came in here telling me that she was looking for a man. I told her so was I. She saw you during the first show and then she asked if I would introduce you. I told her that I would see what I could do."

"V, I don't know if it was the liquor or the love talking last night either way I gotta slow this thing way down and I already know that woman ain't gonna like what I have to say."

"You ain't telling nothing but the truth. She's liable to go buck wild on you. You better watch your back." Joe nodded and sipped his drink.

Later that night at the club, Joe sipped his drink and broached the subject. "Uh Edwina, we need to talk about you movin' in. I don't want us to get off on the wrong foot or nothing but I been doing some thinking. I think we should slow things down a bit and get to know each other a little better before you move in. You know come over and formally get to know my daughter."

Edwina sipped her drink calmly and popped the stale gum in her mouth in silence. Joe stared down at his drink swirling it around in his glass waiting for the fireworks to begin. Finally she said, "Excuse me Suga." She touched his hand. "Can you get me a glass of water?" He got up to get it. She pulled a small bottle out of her pocketbook and poured a few drops in his drink. When he returned, she smiled at him and said, "So what are you going to sing for me tonight?"

He immediately began talking about his song and act for the opening show. Edwina listened to his conversation and patted her hand on her pocketbook. The subject of moving in didn't come up the rest of the night.

The next morning Joe woke up the same as he had the day before only this time Wendy didn't walk in on them. I must be losing my mind, he thought. God knows I miss Viv like hell. Maybe it's taken its toll on me. I gotta stop drinking so much. I'm probably getting so wasted between shows that I subconsciously think that she's Viv. Every morning that week, he woke up with a hang over and Edwina by his side giving him more details about her move into his place. When he would think about their evenings, he would always remember a mention of her not moving in but then he could never remember the rest of the conversation. Pretty soon he realized that the move was settled.

By the end of the week, Joe sat down and told the news to Wendy. "You what? Daddy, who is this woman?" Wendy stared at him as if he had gone crazy. Joe didn't know himself. He stuttered.

"Baby girl, she's a good woman. She has a daughter too. Her name is Regina. She's a couple years older than you. She'll be like a big sister to you," Joe said calmly.

"Whoa, the daughter is movin' in too? It's getting crowded in here ain't it? Maybe I'd better look into staying on campus."

"No, I want you here. We've got plenty of room in this house," he demanded. Wendy sat with her arms folded across her chest. "You made this sound like some fling. You didn't make it sound serious a couple of days ago. How could you? You probably were sleeping with her when Ma was still alive!" Wendy got up and rushed out of the room.

"WENDY!" he yelled. A few seconds later, he heard her slam the door to the roof.

Tears ran down her face as she looked up at the sky. She missed her mother so much. After awhile, she began to feel calm and she realized that her tears were gone from her face as if she had never cried. She smiled. She knew that her mother was there with her. Wendy began to sing. Her mother used to love to listen to her practice her solos for the choir. Singing always took her away from her troubles and they always left a smile on her face. She was on a roll today, she heard Ms. Baker one of the neighbors yell, "Girl, you blow that song. Yes indeed."

After the argument, she and Joe didn't say much to each other in passing. They pretty much stayed out of each others way, that is until the day that Edwina moved in. Edwina and

Regina didn't lift a finger from the time they stepped in the front door. They walked around like they were the new owners of the house. Wendy heard bits and pieces of their conversation as she brought their things inside, "Oh yes, this will definitely have to go to the Salvation Army. We probably need to have a yard sale."

Who do they think that they are? They haven't been in here an hour yet and they're already talking about getting rid of our things, Wendy thought to herself.

That night Wendy couldn't fall asleep. Regina snored like a man with sinus trouble. She finally got up and fell asleep on the couch watching T.V. The next morning, she got up and made her breakfast. Regina came in the kitchen sniffing around within minutes. "Do you mind if I have a taste?" Wendy breathed real hard.

"I guess you can have a taste."

Once Regina sat at the table with her food, she started grazing in her plate as if she was a piece of cattle. From the first bite, she hummed until all of the food was gone. "Regina, would you mind helping me with the dishes?" Wendy asked since it was still her job to do the dishes.

"Sorry I don't wash dishes, cause I got a bad back." Wendy noticed that Edwina and Regina didn't do anything around the house except lie around and eat up any food that Wendy cooked.

The next day, Wendy was sitting at the bar when V came into work that afternoon. "To what do we owe this pleasure?"

"I'm waiting for my Pops."

"It must be an emergency if you couldn't wait to talk to him at home. Anything that I can help with?"

"Do you know any human exterminators? Cause I sure could use one."

"I heard that. Your pops told me a week ago what was going on at your house?"

"V, I gotta get out of there. Those two heffas aint' trying to lift a finger to do nothing. They act like that's what I'm there to do."

"Girl, listen you know your daddy is still mourning the death of your mother deep down inside. He don't even realize it. Be patient with him through these mistakes. He'll eventually see that they're using him. Instead of letting them get on your nerves, why don't you put that energy to use and come on down here and work with us."

"What's this I hear? The word work and Wendy used in the same sentence," Chris Adams, the club owner's son walked up on their conversation. Wendy playfully pushed him as he smiled at her.

"Wouldn't you like to see Wendy's smiling face working with us around here?" V said. Chris looked up at the ceiling as if he were thinking hard about V's question.

"I don't know V." He shook his head still looking at the ceiling. "Number one," Chris held up one of his fingers, "she's used to her daddy taking care of her. Number two," he held up another finger, "she doesn't look like the hard working type. She seems to be more of the spoiled, whining type. You know the kind used to giving orders but not taking them." She punched him in the arm. "Ouch" he rubbed his arm. "Number three, she has a tendency towards violence." Chris shook his head while he rubbed his arm. "Based on those three things V, I don't think that I can answer your question positively."

V had his hands on his hips. "Boy, you don't run this place yet. This ain't up to you, it's up to me and Bessie." Bessie was the kitchen manager at the club. "As a matter of fact, ain't you got somewhere to be at this very second? You need to get busy setting up the dining room for that birthday party."

"I'm on it, V. So I'll check you later." He touched Wendy's arm and gave her a seductive glance as he walked away.

"Now Wendy give it a shot, you could make a little money helping us out around here while your pops works things out at home." She nodded. "Go in the back and tell Ms. Bessie that I said to give you an apron and plenty to do."

"Baby girl, what's this I hear about you?" Joe demanded.

"I need to make some money to move out on my own," Wendy said while she was waiting for V to fill her tables drink order.

"What you talking about?" Joe frowned.

"You know the saying there can be only one woman running a house. After momma died, that was my role. Now that Edwina's moved in, I think it's time for me to move on."

"Your mother and I wanted you to have a good education. We agreed that you would live with us until you finished school. I still expect that to happen. I'll talk to Edwina tonight. So don't you go making plans, you hear?" She nodded her head. She didn't have enough money to make any immediate plans. She knew that she had no choice but to go with the flow for the moment.

Every time Joe started to bring Wendy up in conversation with Edwina that night at the club, she would start fidgeting. She got up and went to the bathroom. Wendy walked out of one of the bathroom stalls to find Edwina examining a small bottle. She's probably on drugs was the first thought that flashed through Wendy's mind. I better watch leaving any money lying around at the house. Edwina looked in the bathroom mirror and there stood Wendy watching her. She put the bottle in her bag. "Your father know you here?"

"Yep"

"So what you standing there staring at me for?"

"I'm wondering what he could possibly see in you."

"Why you little ungrateful…" Wendy walked out the door before she could finish the sentence.

Enough was enough. She had to tell her father what was going on. She saw him on stage. Within seconds, Joe fainted on stage in front of his audience.

"Daddy, are you okay?" Wendy said with tear-streaked eyes. She was the first person that Joe saw when he opened his eyes in his hospital room. Joe patted her hand and smiled.

"Yes baby girl, I'm O.K, " he said with a husky voice. It felt like it took all his strength just to rest his hand on hers. "Sure do wish that your mama was here right now. I miss her so much". His voice trailed off as he closed his eyes and silent tears rolled down his face. Wendy sat by his side and sang softly to him until he finally drifted off to sleep.

When Wendy left the hospital her mind was racing. She didn't tell her father about last night. He was dealing with enough at the moment. She knew that she needed to kick that crack head and her daughter out of the house. She was going to need help doing that. Maybe she could get T-Bone and Eddie, the bouncers at the club to help her do it. But then she knew she would need somebody there to make sure that they didn't break in and steal anything. Her head was scrambled. The doctors were going to run tests on her father to find out what was wrong with him. She got on the bus and headed to V's house. She needed some good advice. He could help her figure this out. She had just rung the bell on the bus for V's stop when she saw Edwina going into the House of Meditations. V lived just above the store.

What was Edwina doing going into the House of Meditations? People went to Esther, the store owner and V's landlord if they needed healing or if they wanted to place a spell on someone. Wait a minute. Wendy's mind flashed back to the other night when she bumped into Edwina in the bathroom. She hadn't seen any rocks in that bottle. It could have been one of Esther's potions. She made it up the back steps to V's unnoticed.

She knocked on his door. "Well look what the cat brought home," he said as he opened the door to let her in. She told V her story. "I'll talk to Esther and see what I can find out. In the meantime, you need to stay away from your house while your pops is gone. It's no telling what other stuff that woman may have brought from Esther to get rid of you. If you don't have anywhere to go, you are more than welcome to stay here until we get this all figured out. As a matter of fact, I would prefer it. I'm gettin' too old and tired to be worried about where you living while your pops is in the hospital."

That afternoon, she was singing to herself trying to forget about her troubles while at work. "Girl, with a voice like that, what are you are doing working in the kitchen?" Chris walked up from behind her. "You need to be in the show." Wendy blushed.

"So hurry up and finish college so that you can be my agent. "

"Alright, we can be rich together. I like that," He nodded, "Maybe, I was wrong. You're not so spoiled after all. How about this, I'll finish college and run the club with you by my side running the show. That way I can take care of your daddy's princess, the way she needs to be treated. Like a star." He stared down at her. Wendy blushed. "So for now just keep creating those songs and practicing them on me." V loudly cleared his throat. Chris winked at her and left.

"Look Miss, your daddy ain't here and I sure don't know how to be one," V said loudly since he had caught the look exchanged between them.

"He's so cute," Wendy said, then she smiled.

"Girl, monkeys are cute," V waved his hand at her.

"V, leave the girl alone. Chris is a nice boy. I'd rather see Wendy with him than some of these other characters that come up in here," Bessie fussed at V.

"Okay. Bessie, stop fussing. One thing I give the boy credit for. He has an ear for talent. This girl definitely needs to be in the show," V said.

The third Wednesday each month was amateur night at the club. "Here's your big chance, girl," V encouraged her. "Do you think so?" she was excited about the thought.

"I know so," V signed her up. Wendy told Chris that she was going to be in the show. He told her that he wouldn't miss it. Between school, work and practicing for the show, she didn't have much time to worry about Edwina. She would worry about her when she found out the details from V. She made sure that she went to see her father everyday with a smile on her face no matter how bad he looked some days.

"V, what am I going to wear for the show? I don't have much money."

"Girl, don't worry about a thing, give me your best pair of shoes and your best dress and I'll take care of the rest, free of charge. I've got a friend who owes me a favor. Just remember me when you get famous."

Wendy walked out of the dressing room on amateur night ready for the world with a smile on her face. V had come through as promised. Her outfit and shoes were perfect. She walked on stage amidst loud cheers and whistles to her introduction. There, sitting directly in front of her, was Chris. She opened her mouth and sang as if they were the only two in the entire room. She finished to a standing ovation. Chris met her backstage with a dozen long stem roses and a card, which said, "I want to take our relationship to another level. Let's discuss it over dinner. Love C."

"Let's get out of here," he whispered in her ear.

As they were leaving the club, they walked right into Edwina. "Girl, you getting off early tonight, ain't cha?" Edwina looked her up and down. "You been spending some of your daddy's money?" Edwina asked accusingly.

"What do you want?" Wendy sucked her teeth.

"When your father gets home, I'm going to have a talk with him about your little attitude problem." Edwina folded her arms across her chest.

"That's fine with me, cause he's certainly going to hear an earful from me about you and your daughter. " Wendy frowned and turned to Chris. "Let's get outta here."

"You ain't going nowhere with him," Edwina placed her hand on Wendy's shoulder. "You're coming with me."

Wendy turned to face her. "Get your hands off of me. You are not my mother and don't you ever forget it."

Edwina puffed up and stuck out her chest. "Listen hear chile, in your father's absence, you do what I tell you." They were drawing a crowd. T-Bone and Eddie pushed through the crowd. They grabbed Edwina once they saw that she had her hand on Wendy. That set Edwina off even more. She started swinging her arms at them yelling, "Get your hands off of me!"

Wendy felt an arm grabbing her out of nowhere. When she turned she saw it was V with Esther. "Come on, we need to talk to Esther," V said seriously.

"But Chris and I were going out."

"Tell Chris you'll see him later." She told Chris that she had to leave and that she would explain later.

Esther had come down to the club to catch a glimpse of Edwina to make sure that she knew the proper identity of the woman that V had asked her about. Esther told them that Edwina had come to her looking for a potion that would get her a man. The potion was effective and unharmful when given in the proper dosage. Esther told them that it sounded as if Edwina had been poisoning Joe's system by giving him too much of the potion. Esther gave Wendy an herb that would counteract the potion in Joe's system. Esther let Wendy know in no uncertain terms that she was never to tell anyone of their conversation and if she did then she would suffer the consequences. She knew enough about Esther to know that she was no one to ignore. Within 24 hours of giving Joe Esther's herb, he began to show signs of his old self. Wendy told Joe about Edwina's bottle. Joe remembered seeing the bottle but he didn't think that it contained so much power. He felt relieved to know he hadn't been losing his mind. V and Wendy told him to rest assured that they would take care of getting rid of Edwina and Regina.

Chris walked up on Wendy that afternoon. "I hear that your dad is coming home soon. If you need any help, I'm your man." He grabbed her hand and looked in her eyes.

"I could use your help." They discussed their plans and just as he was leaving to get back to work, he snapped his fingers.

"Oh before I forget, I have this for you." He handed her an envelope. She searched his face and his face remained blank. She opened it and read the letter inside. She hugged him after she read it. "I talked to my dad. I want to hear you sing to me and only me every night from now on. Do we have a deal?"

She kissed him. "Promise me one thing, you'll be sitting in the front."

He smiled and shook his head. "Bet."

The day of Joe's discharge, Wendy and V came to pick him up from the hospital. As they pulled up to the house, Chris, T-Bone and Eddie had just finished putting Edwina and Regina's things at the curb. V took out an aerosol can and sprayed it around the door trim, while the others helped Joe get settled inside. Everyone knew what was to come.

Wendy had been a little nervous about confronting Edwina but she calmed down suddenly once inside. She knew instantly that her mother was in the house. It's working. She thought to herself. Edwina and Regina ain't gonna know what hit them. They were all sitting around the kitchen table catching Joe up on things that had been going on at work when Edwina put the key in the door. "Regina, what's that smell?"

"I don't know Ma but it stinks." Regina walked into the kitchen. She gasped, "Who is that woman?" Everyone was silently watching. Edwina and Regina were under the influence of Esther's spray. They screamed and ducked. Vivian's spirit was flying around them. The spray had awakened Vivian's spirit unexpectedly and she was not happy about it. She knew that these women had tried to take advantage of her family. Now it was her job to let them know that they were not welcome in her home.

Edwina walked in the kitchen and screamed. "Baby, get your things, it's Joe's wife Vivian. She's madder than a hornet. We gotta get outta here now!" Joe got up from the table and walked towards them slowly. "Don't come near me." Edwina yelled and then she ran to the front door. Joe kept coming towards them. He started smiling. He was enjoying watching their reaction. Regina was slower than her mother. "Ma!" she screamed. "She's flying through me. Open the door! We gotta get out of here!" The front door was locked. Edwina was so flustered she couldn't unlock the door. Regina was so freaked out by Vivian's spirit that she started crying and banging on the front door. "Open the door! She's howling that we'd better leave and never return. Hurry, open the door." Edwina finally got the door open. They stumbled out onto the street. Joe stood in the window laughing at them as they stared back with surprised looks on their faces from time to time. Once they had disappeared up the street, everyone in the house laughed and hollered. They all knew that they wouldn't have to worry about seeing Edwina and Regina again.

First Time for Everything

"Whew! It's hot in here." I said out loud. I opened my eyes to bright sunlight peeking through my closed bedroom blinds and my night gown sticking to my body like it's my second skin. The bed sheet is on the floor and I'm lying diagonally across the bed. What the hell was I doing last night, I thought to myself, as I get up and go to the bathroom. As I sit on the toilet getting my head together, I hear the sound of woodchimes knocking in the room, as if there are woodchimes hanging up in my bathroom. However, there are no chimes at all hanging up in my bathroom. As a matter of fact, my windows aren't open and the sound isn't coming from outside or in. I've heard this sound before and I've given it a name. I call it the sound of my soul. I've heard it in my sleep before and I've heard it in a room full of people and I know that I'm the only one that hears that sound. It is a beautiful, mellow, earthy, happy sound and I'm old enough to know what it means when I hear it. I smile at the thought of its meaning.

Ever since I can remember, whenever I hear the sound of my soul it means that a lover is about to walk into my life that very day. I smile at the memory of past loves. Be it one night stands, two month lovers, two year lovers, or an occasional lover, whenever I hear the sound of my soul before the clock strikes midnight, my prince will appear. It's like a sixth sense, an itch that needs to be scratched. Some have been boyfriends, some have become boyfriends, some were just acquaintances, one or two strangers when I was younger. Some were even married and I didn't know it at the time cause I don't believe in getting busy with a married man. My motto on married men is if they cheat on their wife, they'll cheat on you. So don't even touch'em. My mind drifts and I realize what day it is. It's my grandbaby, Sydney's first birthday. I smile and get up from the toilet and go into the bedroom and glance at the clock. Oh my God! I've slept in late. It's 11:30 am. Her birthday party starts at 1 pm. I gotta get up. I need to hurry up. I begin my daily morning ritual. I put on the hot water for my tea and I meditate to the good Lord while I wait for the water to get hot. This is just what I need to relax so that I don't go to Syd's party all worked up and out of sorts cause I know that I'm meeting a new lover today and I start getting anxious cause I ain't getting none right now anyway. After I shower, I feel a little better and just as I sit on the bed the phone rings.

"Mommie, why are you still home?" my daughter Nina says in an annoying tone. I smile. What would I do without my drill sergeant. "Is everything okay?" She persists.

"I'm fine." I smile.

"Are you sure?" My daughter thinks she's the boss of me sometimes.

"Does it sound like I'm not okay?" I frown. Okay it's time for me to put an end to the drill sergeant tone of this conversation.

"If I'm not supposed to be home, then why are you calling me?" I ask with slight attitude. Now Nina breathes heavy. The drill sergeant routine has been halted.

"Ma, Malik forgot to get ice. Can you stop at the store and get some, please?"

"Sure baby, what else do you need?" I ask as I reach for my jeans.

"I need you to hurry up and get here. Hold on a minute." I hear a door closing on the other end of the phone. "Uncle Charles is here with his new white girlfriend. He and Aunt Pearl got into a fight about it," Nina whispers.

"What? What's the girlfriend's name? I was curious.

"I don't know, Ginger. No wait it's Mary Ann. That's it." I burst out laughing at Nina's response.

"Where did he get her from? Gilligans Island?" I laughed. Nina laughed at my response.

"Naw, Ma. This Mary Ann don't look innocent and pure enough to be on Gilligans Island. She looks seasoned."

"Oh, what you trying to say, she likes pepper?" I laugh.

"Naw, she looks seasoned like she played in an X-rated version of Gilligan's Island." Nina laughs. "I'm serious. Uncle Charles and Aunt Pearl started arguing and getting loud." I realize that she's serious cause I know how my relatives can be. I breathe heavy at the thought of what she's going to tell me.

"Nina, it's only 1:30. They're fighting already?" My mind flashes to my Aunt Pearl and Uncle Charles. They are my mother's sister and brother. Uncle Charles is a Vietnam vet. He thinks he's a pimp, always has. He's known for dating some skanky women. My Aunt Pearl is my mother's oldest sister. We call her Boss Hog behind her back. She is the second oldest in their family and she is the family matriarch in the true sense. She is 75 and feisty as ever. There is a 20 year age difference between her and my Uncle Charles who is the baby of my mother's family. She tries to boss everyone around. No one is immune to hearing Aunt Pearl's opinions. My parents have both passed and Aunt Pearl and Uncle Charles are the closest relatives logistically to Nina and myself.

"Aunt Pearl asked me real loud who that white lady was like she's deaf or something as soon as they got here. Everybody in the living room heard her so Uncle Charles introduced his girlfriend to her. The girl held out her hand and Aunt Pearl frowned at the girl like she stunk. In Aunt Pearl's defense, the girl came in here with her big boobs stuffed in a halter top two sizes too small and a mini skirt. Aunt Pearl wouldn't even shake the girl's hand."

"She was probably scared to touch her," I responded.

"Then Aunt Pearl looked at Uncle Charles and told him that he must have lost his mind cause she knew that her little brother would never date poor white trash." I just closed my eyes and shook my head. "Then Aunt Pearl said that she needed to leave cause she couldn't stand looking at no stank looking white trash sitting uninvited in her nieces house. Ma, before I could say anything, Uncle Charles told her that she needed to leave cause nobody wanted to see her there anyway. He told her that the only reason she was invited was out of pity cause she didn't have no friends, no life, no nothing cause she's too damn bossy. He told her that she was going to die a lonely bitter old lady just like she had lived a lonely bitter old maid. Then he told her that she needed a man a long time ago but she was too damn bossy and no man was willing to put up with her. He said to top it off, she was too damn old and ugly to even think about getting a man at this point of her life. Ma, Help! This is Sydney's first birthday!"

"Nina, I told you not to invite everybody and their brother to Syd's party. Now didn't I? I said keep it small. But no, you had to make this into a family reunion."

"Ma, can you hurry with the ice, please? I need you," she whined.

"Did Aunt Pearl or Uncle Charles leave?"

"After Uncle Charles read Aunt Pearl up one side and down the other to anyone in the room that would listen, he asked for some liquor. He and Skanky, I mean Mary Ann are sitting in the backyard getting toasty."

"Nina, don't tell me you're serving liquor at Syd's party."

"Ma, you know I know better. We got some wine coolers and beer sitting in a tub full of ice in the backyard." My relatives. We all got some characters in our family, don't we?

"What about Aunt Pearl?"

"She's sitting in the living room, preaching to Janice on how she needs to raise her kids.

"I'm on my way." My grandbaby, Sydney Lashawn Gordon was born in the dog days of summer a year ago on August 26th. Nina's hormones were volcanic during her pregnancy. Her husband Malik and I should be nominated for sainthood based on the hours of anger, tears and discomfort that Nina put us through during her pregnancy. Malik and Nina were married 4 years before having a child. So Malik knew Nina well enough to know that her hormones were off the chart. Sydney inherited Nina's moodiness that she had during the pregnancy. Sydney could laugh and light up an entire room, but when she was upset her facial expression and tears more than showed her displeasure, even though she's young. The temperature hit 102 a year ago while Malik and I were in the labor room helping Nina bring Syd into the world. Today, the temperature was quickly approaching 90 degrees. I could feel the heat inside Nina's house before I even got to the front door. Aunt Pearl was talking my cousin Janice's ear off on the front porch and I could hear Aunt Pearl's voice a couple doors down from Nina's house.

"I can't believe that Charles would have the audacity to bring some poor white trash up in this house," Aunt Pearl said excitedly. "Did you see them out there guzzling drinks down like they're drinking water in front of Nina's friends and their little ones. Her friends must think that we're crazy. We're here to celebrate a birthday party. This is for friends and family. This ain't some bar. They're just disrupting this babies' party." I walked up the steps and they were so engrossed in their conversation that they didn't realize that I was there."

"Well Hello Aunt Pearl. Hi Janice." I smiled at both of them as they looked up. We hugged and kissed.

"Tina, you look too young to be a grandmother," Janice remarked.

"Why thank you." I blush at the comment.

"She does, doesn't she?" Aunt Pearl chimes in. "Girl, you must be living right." We all laughed. "T, Charles is sitting in the backyard disrespecting Nina's house. He's back there drunk, looking like Superfly with some poor white trash that he looks like he picked up on the corner before he got here." Aunt

Pearl said disgusted. Janice frowned and shook her head in agreement. I glanced at them.

"Really?"

"Go see for yourself," Aunt Pearl said. "We'll be sitting right here."

"I'll be back," I said as I open the door and go in the house. No one is in the living room nor the dining room which had happy birthday streamers coming from the ceiling with decorative plates and cups around a birthday cake. I proceed to the kitchen and there is my baby, Nina, seasoning hamburger patties at the sink with my niece Natalie adding ginger ale to the punch. "Hello Ladies." I smile.

"Hi Aunt Tina. Perfect timing. I'll take those bags of ice."

"Thank you, alright Boo what you want me to do."

"Ma, can you help us start bringing the food outside?" I can smell hamburgers cooking on the grill coming thru the screen door in the kitchen. The backyard is full of people. Babies and their parents from Sydney's daycare are sitting under the old shady oak trees in Nina's backyard. I see some of Nina's college friends, Wanda and Gloria with their husbands and kids. There are some cousins that I haven't seen in years and Nina's in-laws along with Malik's sisters, their families and his uncle who happens to be a Vietnam vet. There is Uncle Charles holding court with Janice's teenage sons and some of their friends. Uncle Charles' girlfriend is talking to…wait a minute! I know that's not who I think it is. Nina snuck one over on me. There was my baby's daddy, Mo, talking to Uncle Charles' girlfriend. Now I could see why everyone was using the term, skanky when they talked about this woman. She was skinny and her breast was bursting out of the seams of her top. To top it off, she had stringy hair. Now I understood why Aunt Pearl was calling her poor white trash. Music is playing. It was a full fledged party. Just as I put food on the table, OPP came on and I started dancing. Malik's uncle, Eric started dancing with me. I did a spin and I started dancing with my behind facing him and when I turned around to face him, he was dancing with Mary Ann who came up behind him and I'm dancing face to face with my Nina's daddy. I can't believe this. I haven't seen Mo since Nina's wedding five years ago. "Damn, he still looks good!" I think to myself. Why didn't that girl tell me that her father was here? Here I was being sarcastic telling her that she had the invite list for a family reunion when this proved my point. I can smell Mo's cologne. He's smiling at me with a devilish look on his face. I smile back. It's getting hot out here under the shade. I need some air. Mo is working it out and I'm giving him something to work for but I need some air. He laughs as the song stops and I let out a nervous laugh. What is wrong with me? He reaches over and hugs me.

"What's up stranger?" he smiled at me with his beautiful green laughing eyes.

"What's up with you? I wasn't expecting to see you here. Nina didn't mention that you were coming."

"It was kind of last minute. I was able to reschedule some things to get out here to celebrate Syd's first birthday. Since I haven't seen Syd since Nina brought her out 6 months ago. I had to see my girl. She's a doll baby isn't she? She's a cutie just like her mother and grandma or should I call you Nana? You look to young to be a grandmother." My mind was blank. All I could think about was how hot it was out here. With the morning that I'd had, his appearance had totally unnerved me. Could I be pre-menopausal or having a hot flash?

"Can you excuse me for a second?"

"Sure".

"Baby girl," Uncle Charles' speech is starting to slur as he staggers towards us.

"Hi Uncle Charles," I smile as he hugs me.

"Baby girl, I want you to meet Mary." He was so drunk that he couldn't even say her name correctly. He is obviously drinking more than a wine cooler. I looked over where he was sitting and there on the table between him and Malik's uncle was a fifth of scotch. His woman was in deep conversation with Malik's uncle. "Mary, come here." The girl seemed to be in a deep private conversation. "Mary, come here right now!" She excused herself and came over. "Mary, I want you to meet my lovely niece, Baby Girl." I raised my hand in a wave before she stuck her hand out. I was still Aunt Pearl's niece, you know.

"Nice to meet you." when she smiled, she showed two front buck teeth.

"Nice to meet you, too."

"Baby Girl, Mary takes care of me." He winked. I had heard enough.

"Uncle Charles, Mary, please excuse me but I need to help Nina get the food set up out here."

"Do you need my help?" Mary Ann offered.

"No, we got everything covered. Just enjoy yourself I'll be back in a few minutes, Uncle Charles." He nodded and began to stagger back to his seat. I rush to the back door. I pass Nina on the back porch bringing more food out of the house.

"Nina?" I say in a low stern voice. Her eyes got big.

"Ma, are you okay?" I let out a frustrated grunt as I went in the house. I headed straight for the bathroom and locked the door. I needed some private time to think. I took a few deep breaths. I can do this. I say to myself. Mo looks too damn good. I can feel my panties getting wet just from the thought.

Maurice Christian and I first met at our alma mater, Norfolk State University. Mo was a member of Kappa Alpha Psi and I was a member of the Alpha Kappa Alpha sorority. Mo was a year ahead of me and when I got to campus, he had already established the reputation of a rich womanizing pretty boy. Originally, we knew each other through mutually social acquaintances and nothing more until me and some of my sorer sisters went to the Greek picnic, the summer of my Junior year. It was in Philadelphia that year. There was this house party that Saturday night in Philly being given by one of the Kappa's from my school, Warren. Everybody called him Spoon because he had a funny shaped head that looked just like a spoon. By the time we got there, the party was jumping. The air in the house was hot and you could smell the weed. Me and my crew went in different directions as soon as we got there. I headed outside in the backyard to breath. Outside, a card game was going on and people were lighting up and just chilling. Over in a corner was Mo. He had the only empty chair next to him so I strolled over.

"Hey Mo, mind if I sit here?" Most of the time when I saw him around campus, he was always with a pretty girl or two. He shook his head no as he puffed on his joint. I had heard he never dated anyone for very long. He was adorable. He had brown curly hair, brown skin, dimples and green slanted eyes that made it look like he was always laughing and whenever he smiled he looked like a mischievous little boy that had done something bad and was trying to get away with it without telling anyone.

"What trouble you getting into tonight?" he asked me as he passed me his joint. I shrugged my shoulders.

"I'm trying to find out what everybody else is doing." He just shook his head as smoke slowly escaped through his lips. I took a puff.

"Girl, the summer looks like it agrees with you. Looks like you're getting a little thick in all the right places." He smiled and nodded.

"What you trying to say, I'm eating too much?" I glanced at him sideways.

"Not at all. Keep doing what you doing. You're looking real good." He licked his lips. "You look so tasty. I think I want to bite you."

I knew by his look that I had just found my trouble for the evening. I looked at him and smiled as he leaned over and kissed me. He was so cute.

He looked me up and down. Like he would eat me up at any moment. "You thirsty?" I shook my head. He handed me a cup beside his chair. I took a sip. Cognac and coke. He put his arm across the back of my chair. I relaxed back in my chair.

"So you and your boys going to step tonight?"

"They might, but I got other trouble that I want to get into tonight." He glanced at me.

"Yeah, what do you have in mind?" He took my hand and rose from his chair.

"Follow me."

Spoon was standing by the stairs leading upstairs. Mo whispered into Spoon's ear. He gave him the nod and we headed upstairs.

"What are you majoring in?" I ask him.

"Engineering." I wasn't expecting to hear that.

"So you coming out this year right?"

"Hell yeah, I'm out of there." He smiled showing that cute dimple.

"I hear that. I wish I was out of there this year." He walked into what seemed to be Spoons' parents' bedroom.

"You are a junior, right?" I shook my head.

"So what you gonna do after you graduate?" I asked.

"I'm moving to the west coast next summer."

"Really?" He shook his head.

"My sister and her family are out there. I got a place to stay and I've got all year to look for a job." We sat on the bed.

"That's exciting, I've never been to the west coast but I've always wanted to go."

"Well, now you'll have somebody to visit when you come out." He kissed me and this electric current went through my body and I heard the woodchimes for the first time in my life. At the time, I didn't think anything of it. I just knew that I felt mellow and reflective like I was exactly where I was supposed to be at that point in time. Someone turned on a boombox in the backyard just below our bedroom window. Aqua Boogie was rattling the bedroom windows.

"Oh that's my jam right there." His head started bobbing. "Come on and dance with me." I realized when we got up to dance how high I was. I wasn't feeling any pain and neither was he. We were having a ball. Mo was right behind me move for move. "Go ahead, girl and work that thing. You know how I like it." I smiled and glanced back and at him and our eyes locked. He was feeling me. "Yeah, give me what you got." At that point, he grabbed my waist and pulled me back on the bed and we got busy. I was so high that I felt like I was in another world. I heard the woodchimes more than once that night. I had never had an out of body experience, but you couldn't tell me that I wasn't flying that night and I was feeling Mo. He rocked my world. I knew his style so I knew that even though we got busy that night, I needed to play it cool when we got back to school. I couldn't sweat him even though I'll admit whenever I saw him when we were back on campus that Fall I always stared at him longer than usual. Anytime, he saw me, he always gave me plenty of love and attention. He treated me like a long lost lover. I loved every minute of it. We hung out a couple of times. Once, he happened to be on campus in his TR-6 and he asked me if I wanted to see his new place. I hopped right in his ride. He had a nice off campus bachelor pad with another of his frat brothers. We got busy but again knowing his type, I knew there were no strings attached. It seemed that the more I treated him as a casual friend, the more he befriended me. He was fine, funny and great in bed. I wasn't sleeping with anyone else at the moment and I figured why get stressed about not having a serious relationship when this was more fun. Then that October, he came to scoop me up for a ride down to the beach on a beautiful Indian summer day. My period was about 3 weeks late. I was worried. He had packed a blanket and he had bought us sandwiches and wine for a picnic on the beach. It was so romantic. While we were laying on the blanket enjoying the ocean and sunshine, I told him my predicament. He was cool. "Did you take a pregnancy test yet?" I shook my head no. "Well, let's find out." I gave him a pitiful look. He held my hand and looked me in the eye. "Let's find out today." I shook my head o.k. On the way home from the beach, I bought a test and we went back to his house.

"If it's positive, I'm having it." I stared at the stick waiting for it to change color. "I don't believe in abortion."

"We'll deal with it. Let's find out first." He was silent. I held up the stick after I saw that it was positive. He was silent.

After a few minutes of silence, I said "Don't you have anything to say?" He breathed deep.

"We'll deal with it." He took me home that night and I figured that was goodbye, until he came to see me that following Saturday. "Are you sure that you want to have this baby?" He looked me dead in the eye.

"I couldn't be more sure about anything," I said confidently.

"What about us?" He looked at me.

"You're my baby's daddy that's what I think about us." I wanted more but I needed him to tell me that we had a chance of being more.

"Is that it? I don't want you getting the wrong idea thinking that I'm going to marry you because of this." I shook my head no. I was sad but I knew from the beginning what I was dealing with and I knew more than anything that I needed to stay strong for the baby's sake. He watched my reaction. "I'll be there for our child, but I'm still moving to the west coast when I graduate." That cut like a knife but I knew what I was getting into at the time.

During homecoming weekend, Mo introduced me to his parents. He had told me that week that he had told them about me and they wanted to meet me. His mother was strikingly beautiful. She had green laughing eyes just like her son. I met them at his apartment.

She looked me up and down and then she smiled. "Come take a walk with me." We walked around Mo's complex just the two of us. "So Mo tells me that I'm going to be a grandmother." She smiled. "When is my grandchild's birthday?" She said in a happy tone.

"June 7th," I smiled.

"That's great news, my birthday is June 10th. How are you planning to take care of the baby? Are you going to drop out?" This woman asked me more questions about my future than her own son had ever asked me.

"I'm planning to come back to school and finish next year after the baby's born.

"I would like to help." She watched my face for my expression. My facial expression was blank. "May I ask you a question?" She stopped walking, faced me and held both of my hands in hers. "Why don't you let me take care of the baby after its born?" I couldn't believe what she was saying. "I know that you don't know me and this isn't a trick. But this is my grandchild and I can afford to give this child the best care.

"Mrs. Christian, I appreciate your offer. But honestly, I don't know you. That's asking a lot to take care of someone's child. I mean, I've just met you."

"Think about it. You can come and visit whenever you want. You can live with us. Mo is leaving in May, moving to the west coast. You and the baby can move right in. I'll take care of the baby while you're at school. Please think about it. My husband and I can take care of the baby's every need."

"Mrs. Christian, I appreciate your offer. But me and the baby are going to live with my parents. My mom is going to take care of the baby while I'm here finishing my senior year."

Mrs. Christian had a sad look in her eye for a split second and then she said "I don't want to be a stranger to my grandchild. Come visit with me now and get to know me so that you'll feel comfortable one day bringing my grandchild to visit me." She squeezed my hands and turned them loose. Mo and I went to visit his parents one weekend before the Fall Semester ended. Their house was something out of an Ebony magazine. It looked like a movie stars home. Mrs. Christian went out of her way to make sure that my every need was met. I still had feelings for Mo. He treated me like a queen. We had fun together however, he made it clear that we were just having a child together and that he was going to California once he graduated and that he intended to always be in his child's life. I saw his parents a few more times before Nina was born. I knew the day that Nina was coming into this world. I woke up to the sound of woodchimes. Nina LaShawn Roberts was born into this world on the same day as her paternal grandmother. She came into this world with her father and grandmother's green laughing eyes. She was beautiful. True to Mo's word by the time Nina was born, he was living in California. I called him and his mom and told them about Nina. His parents came to see Nina that summer and they met my parents. They stayed in touch as Mo's mom wanted and by the time Nina was 9. She was visiting Mo on the West Coast at least two weeks out of every summer. Mo never did marry. He lived with a couple of women from time to time. I never married either. I guess I just became too set in my ways over time and I never developed the patience to tolerate living with another person outside of Nina for long. After having Nina, my whole world became about her. I would date and have the occasional boyfriend but Nina came first. I didn't regret one thing. I smiled at the thought. A knock on the bathroom door brought me back to reality.

"I'm coming out in a second." I opened the bathroom door to see someone hugged up with Mary Ann next to the bathroom door and it wasn't Uncle Charles. I peeked a little harder. It was Malik's Uncle Eric. I cleared my throat for attention but neither looked at me. As I walked towards the kitchen, I heard the bathroom door shut and I turned around to find both of them gone. I took a deep breath and knocked on the bathroom door before I got any response I said "Listen, this is my daughter's house. I don't know what you think you're going to do in there but regardless of that get out of there." I walked towards the kitchen waiting to hear the sound of the door open. It did. I didn't even bother looking back as I heard foot steps heading towards the front of the house. I opened the back door to go back outside. Nina was standing on the porch. "Nina, Uncle Charles date was trying to get busy with Uncle Eric in your bathroom." She looked shocked. Malik's Uncle Eric had never been quite right since coming back from Vietnam so neither of us was even surprised.

Just then, Janice walked up behind us. "I see Uncle Charles' woman is working the party. I saw her walk up the street with Malik's uncle. We all looked over at Uncle Charles. He was dancing with any female that he could find. He was having a ball.

Just then, he yelled for us. "Nina, Tina, come on down here. We're about to do the electric slide. We all headed down the steps as most of the party got up to dance. I was right in between Mo and Nina. Janice realized this and said that we had to get a picture. We were all game. Mo stood with his arms around both of us. Then Malik joined us with Sydney. I started getting hot again. This time Mo must have sensed my apprehension cause after we took pictures, he grabbed my hand. "Come on and sit over here so we can catch up. So what's been going on with you these days, T? You look fantastic." His laughing eyes shot up and his dimple appeared.

"So do you."

"So, who's the boyfriend? Is he here or is that too personal?"

I shook my head no and smiled. "I'm enjoying my freedom these days. I'm not seeing anyone special."

"What about you? Are you still dating that model? What was her name? Madonna or LaDonna?"

"LaDonna and no I'm not dating her anymore. I'm an old man now. I don't have the time, patience or physical endurance to date these young girls." He frowned like he had hurt a body part. I laughed at his expression.

"She didn't seem like she was that young."

"Let's just say, she was two years older than Nina and she was dumb as a stump but she was gorgeous. I need a woman who knows who she is. No more girls."

"Look who's growing up," I said surprised. He laughed. "I've been grown ever since you got pregnant with Nina." I looked at him like he was crazy.

"Mo, I'm glad to see you so don't sit here and act like a stump. Let's just say, that you've grown up since I saw you at Nina's wedding cause you bought LaDonna to the wedding."

"Point taken, I'll give you that." Just then our song came on, Aqua Boogie. Uncle Charles was still out there dancing. I don't think he even knew that his girlfriend was no longer at the party. I flashed back to that night when Nina was conceived in Spoons parents bed. Next, we danced to Always and Forever. During that dance, Mo let me know that he was feeling me and I let him know that I was feeling him. I wasn't nervous anymore. A sense of calm had come over me. I excused myself afterwards and I let him know that I would be back. I went in the kitchen to help Nina with the cake and ice cream.

"Ma, what are you and daddy doing out there?" I smiled.

"Just a little sumthing, why?"

"Ma! You and daddy?" she frowned. I laughed. Kids can never imagine their parents having sex.

"We had you didn't we?" Then she laughed.

"Okay but can you tone it down a little. I'm embarrassed. You and daddy are out there acting like two inseparable love birds and you're embarrassing me."

"Oh Nina, get over it."

"Let me hurry up and serve this cake and ice cream before my parents end up doing it in my backyard." We both burst out laughing at the thought. As we sang Happy Birthday to Sydney, she laughed and her green eyes shined just like her mom, grandfather, and great grandmother. After we sang Happy Birthday to Sydney and everyone had dessert, people began to pack up and leave. Uncle Charles started asking if anyone had seen his date. I told him that I hadn't seen her, which wasn't a lie cause I hadn't seen her in quite awhile. He went into the house and Aunt Pearl was on the front porch. Before he could say anything, she pointed down the street and said, "Your piece of trash left and went down the street with some guy from the backyard."

"What?" Uncle Charles frowned.

"You heard me, you old fool. She don't want you. She found her another man to take care of her."

"Mind your business, heffa. She works for me and she's working today."

"Lord Jesus" Aunt Pearl started fanning herself.

"Uncle Charles!" I hollered. "I know you not starting no trouble in my daughter's house now, right?"

"T, I was minding my own business when she started dipping into my damn business."

"Okay then leave her alone. Just don't say any more to her." He looked over at Aunt Pearl and waved his arm dismissing her and he walked down the street in the direction that Aunt Pearl had pointed. Mo and I stayed after most were gone. Mo played with Sydney and talked to Malik and some of their friends while I helped Nina clean up. Afterwards, I was tired and decided to go home. I kissed Nina and Syd. I knew that Mo and I were going to hook up but I didn't want to upset Nina by leaving with him, since I figured we had disrupted her party enough with our actions.

"It was good seeing you, Mo." He frowned at my actions. I hugged him, grabbed his hands, and handed him a note. He held on to the note and put it in his pocket unnoticed. In the note I told him to give me a 10 minute lead time to get out of there and I gave him my address and phone number. Our drill sergeant was watching our every move.

"You leaving?" Mo asked sincerely.

"Yeah, I'm going home to put my feet up."

"I might call you before I leave."

"I'll be home." Nina was listening to our every word. We hugged again and I left. I got home with enough time to change into something comfortable just before the doorbell rung. I opened the door and he walked in and wrapped his arms around me and said "Just what I need a smart, beautiful woman." I could hear the woodchimes in the distance.

No House Calls

1962

"The jury has found the defendant, not guilty your Honor." Pernell Randolph flashed his pearly whites at his attorney.

"Doc, thank you for representing me."

"P, don't mention it. I always knew that one of my church members didn't steal a T.V. from Hall's Department store. Lord knows. These are just some crazy times that we're living in."

"Amen Doc amen. I'll be by to pay you tomorrow."

"I'll see you then." Doc walked out of the courtroom over to the bench just outside. He placed his hand on the shoulder of a woman sitting there with her head down.

"Shirley, are you ready?"

She raised her head. "Doc, I'm ready."

"Good, let's go see how your boy's doing"

"Doc, thank you for taking the time to represent my boy, Ricky. I know that he wasn't involved in looting the liquor store."

He patted her shoulder. "Don't worry, let me hear what he has to say."

Later that morning, as soon as Doc walked into Melvin's Rib Joint, there were three people waiting to ask him advice on their troubles. By the time, he had finished with the last person, his lunch appointment James Crump was waiting. "Doc, I see that business is good."

"You can say that again. As a matter of fact, can you give me a ride to the courthouse after we eat? Ruth needed the car today." James shook his head.

"How's things going for the big time lawyer?" Doc asked his friend.

"I wish I was doing more for my people. I'm handling mostly wills and contracts. Very few trial cases."

"Yeah, but you're raking in the bucks working for big time, Nelson Kane."

"Please, you know Nelson. He's just full of show and he wants to make it look like he cares for our people but the truth is that he really just cares about the almighty dollar."

Doc laughed. "I know. Same old Nelson from law school. He's all flash and no brains. He pays for the brains using his old man's money. I imagine he would have tried to buy me too if I was worth his while," Doc replied.

"You taking the bar again?" James asked.

Doc shook his head. "I don't need that. I got plenty of business without having my license. Thank God, I don't have to be licensed to represent my people in this day and time. Plus

I've gotten used to working on my terms. I don't think that I could work on anyone else's at this point in time."

"Just don't let Nelson Kane get wind of that." James looked serious.

Doc laughed. "I'll put that turkey in his place. If he comes in here messing with me."

"Don't under estimate his power. That's all I'm saying."

"I know. I know."

"Excuse me, Doc." Pernell walked over to their table just as their food arrived.

"Yes Pernell, I want you to meet a good friend of mine." Pernell was black as midnight. He flashed his pearly whites looking in James direction. "This is James Crump. One of the lawyers over at Kane and Associates."

"Oh, you're one of them high priced lawyers." They all laughed.

"Brother, I'm just trying to make some money out here just like you."

"Excuse me, Doc, speaking of money, I came to settle up for my case. I know that you said that you would take whatever I could provide you for your services. I want you to have this." Pernell pushed a large box in front of him on the floor. It was a 20-inch color television.

After a long silence, Doc spoke "I don't know. Your family could use this more than Ruth and I."

Pernell shook his head. "I wouldn't have it any other way. I could have been placed in jail today. If it weren't for you, I might not be seeing my wife and kids tonight. "

Doc let out a sigh.

"I appreciate all you have done for me. You trusted me when some of my own family members had doubts about my troubles. You stuck by me."

"Why thank you, P. I appreciate it but I'm sure that you would have done the same for me."

James tapped his watch. "We'd better hurry if you've got to get to the courthouse soon."

Later that evening Doc's wife Ruth asked him, "Thurmond, what are we going to do with another T.V.?"

"Does your sister need another one?" he asked.

"We've already given her two this year."

"What about the church?"

"We've given them one also. Why don't you just tell folks to give you appliances that we don't have or better yet tell them to give you money?"

"Ruth, I'm just fortunate that people even want me to represent them. Beggars can't be choosers. I'm just glad that I'm busy."

"I know Thurmond. I know."

Doc spent most of the next day at Ricky's pre-trial hearing. He bumped into Nelson Kane at the courthouse. "Well, look who we have here. You pay other people to come down here and do your work for you, right? What happened someone call in sick today?"

Nelson laughed at Doc's comments. "If I had someone like you working for me, then I wouldn't have to be seen in here. I hear that this place is your second home."

Doc nodded. "Some days it feels like it."

"Why don't you come on and work for me. You could put Ruth in a nice big house and a big pretty car. That's what she deserves."

Doc put his head down and laughed. "She's my wife now. She has been for quite a while. Besides, I like making an honest living."

Nelson got a funny look on his face and his tone changed. "You'll see things my way soon enough."

"I doubt it." Doc responded as he turned to head back in to Ricky's pre trial hearing, "Man, get over it." Doc knew that Nelson hated to lose and one of his biggest loses in life was one of Doc's life long gains that would be his wife Ruth. Doc met Nelson and Ruth in law school. Nelson and Ruth were a couple. Nelson's daddy was financing Nelson's education however, Ruth's brains gained her full scholarship monies that financed her education. Nelson turned on his charm when around Ruth however, when he wasn't with her around campus others saw him for what he was, a lying, cheating snake. Doc's honesty, hard work and charm exposed Nelson's traits to Ruth during their first major first year school debate. She realized watching Nelson during that debate that he would lie, cheat and steal to achieve his life long goals. She knew then that she didn't plan to be one on his list of life long goals. She had been with Doc ever since and Nelson had been watching their relationship from afar ever since.

Doc stopped by Melvin's on the way home. There were a couple of people waiting to talk to him. Just as he was getting ready to leave, Melvin yelled from the kitchen. "Doc, wait a minute before I forget. You've been requested to make a house call."

Doc laughed. "Did you tell them that I don't make house calls?"

"I tried to tell that young gal that she needed to come back here tomorrow but she was crying so bad that she was starting to upset my customers so I just took her address. She said to come by tomorrow anytime." Melvin handed Doc the slip of paper. "Oh yeah, Ruth called and said to bring home dinner. Here." Melvin handed Doc two styrofoam containers.

"Did she tell you that she was gonna pay for these dinners?"

"She told me to put it on your tab."

"Didn't I tell you to stop listening to her?"

Melvin waved his hand at him. "Man, go on home. I'm just listening to your boss, that's all."

"Well, don't tell the boss about the house call."

"Man, you think I'm crazy. She'd have my head hanging right next to yours if she knew."

Doc grinned and took the containers and went home. Ruth didn't like him making any house calls. She would never tell him why but she made him promise never to do it.

The following morning, Doc headed out making his first stop the house call. The day was so beautiful that he decided to walk. He passed Pernell along the way. "P, you got rid of all of those T.V's yet?" Doc said in a low voice.

"Now if you know anybody that wants to buy one then please let me know." Doc nodded.

When he reached the address of his house call, a light skinned young woman opened the door. "Mr. Evans, thank you for coming."

Doc bowed his head and took off his hat as he entered her home. "How can I help, Ms?"

"Sarah, please just call me Sarah."

"Do I know your family? You look familiar."

"No, I don't think so. I'm not from these parts. Please have a seat." Doc sat down at the kitchen table. "Would you care for a glass of water?"

"Why yes."

She brought back the water and he took a couple sips as she proceeded to talk. Doc's eyelids suddenly became very heavy. He couldn't make out what she was saying. He couldn't hold his eyes open. He went to sleep.

When he opened his eyes again, it was pouring down raining and he was lying on a cot in what appeared to be an abandoned house. What happened? He thought. Why am I here? He sat up. Ruth must be worried sick. He stood up and his legs immediately collapsed to the floor. He finally stood and staggered around until he finally got his balance. He walked outside of the abandoned house, which was on the outskirts of town. I'd better get home. He walked 3 miles until he reached the bus stop. He placed his hand in his pocket and pulled out thirty-five cents and a bus token. He tried to brush some of the dirt off of his clothes but he was filthy.

The people at the bus stop were smirking at him. He stared at the cars at the traffic light. "What kind of car, is that?" he asked the woman standing closest to him.

"That's a BMW," she said it in a tone like he wasn't quite right in the head.

"That's a mighty fine car." The bus pulled up. He stared at the bus thinking when did we get new buses. He was the last one to get on the bus. He put his token in the bus slot. The bus driver stayed put with the door open. "Excuse me sir, that will be $1.00."

"A dollar? I'm just going to Redwood Street."

"Sir, that will be $1.00 or you'll have to get off of the bus."

"I gave you my bus token."

People on the bus started grumbling. "Come on old man," somebody shouted. Doc dug in his pockets. He had thirty-five cents. He got off of the bus and began walking home.

He knew that something was wrong within two blocks of his walk. There were brand new homes sitting in lots that were vacant yesterday. There were lots of new cars on the street that he had never seen before. Boys were wearing earrings in both ears and their shorts were longer than he had remembered. I'd better go to Melvin's first, he thought. If I go home like this, Ruth is going to start crying.

"Is this the 100 block of North Broad Street?" Doc asked a homeless guy sitting on the curb.

"Yeah" the guy mumbled.

"What happened to Melvin's rib joint?"

The guy stared at Doc. "You're not from around here, are you?"

"What happened to Melvin's?" Doc got anxious.

"Melvin's been closed for about twenty five years now."

"Twenty five years! He was just open yesterday."

"It might seem like yesterday but it was twenty five years ago."

"What year is it now?"

The guy stared at Doc again. "1987"

Doc staggered.

The homeless guy pulled a bottle from his coat and took a drink from it. He wiped off the top and handed it to Doc. "It ain't that much but you look like you sure could use a shot right now."

Doc took the bottle from his friend and sat down next to him. After taking a swig and practically burning a hole in his lung, he asked. "What happened to Melvin's?"

"There was a fella by the name of Doc Evans. He was smart as a whip. The boy was too smart for his britches. He was a dime store lawyer in the community. A lot of folks around here respected him. Anyway, his office was in Melvin's restaurant." Doc took another swig. "While people would wait to talk to Doc, they would order food from Melvin's. One day, Doc turned up missing. That was the strangest thing. They never did find his body. Folks think that the Klan must have got a hold of him. I was one of the last people to see him."

Now Doc stared real hard at the stranger. "Pernell, that you?"

He turned his head to Doc.

"Yeah, how do you know my name?"

"It's me, Doc."

Pernell squinted his eyes and stared at Doc. "If you're Doc, what's the last thing we talked about."

Doc grinned. "I asked you if you'd gotten rid of those T.V.'s yet and you told me that if I knew anyone that wanted to buy one to let you know."

Pernell started laughing. "Doc, where have you been, man?"

Doc told him the bits and pieces that he could remember from that last morning.

"Man, sounds to me like that woman put something on you." Doc nodded.

"Listen old man, walk with me and show me around. Update me on what I've been missing since I've been gone.

Ruth and I will put you up. Plus I might need you to vouch for me in case she don't recognize me," Doc laughed.

"Let's get you to the barbershop so that you can get cleaned up a bit for her at least. Cause man, right now, you look worst than me."

"P, what ever happened to Melvin?"

"Where you think we are going now? After you disappeared, Melvin's customers slowly moved out of the city and stopped coming downtown so he went out of business. Then he took up barbering. Come on."

"Pernell, it's been at least a month of Sundays since I've seen you. Come on and sit down here." Melvin popped the towel that he had in his hand in the barber chair.

"Before you get to me, take care of my man. He's been away for awhile and he's in need of some magic."

Doc stepped forward and Melvin motioned for him to sit in the chair. "So how you want it?"

"Just cut it low."

Melvin started talking to Pernell as he began cutting Doc's hair. "So where you been hiding, man?"

"Believe it or not, I've been staying close by your old place."

"Down there on Broad? I ain't been through there in a long time. Ain't nobody left down there."

"You ever hear what happened to Doc?" Melvin paused with the clippers in his hand.

"Naw, I never heard anything about Doc since he disappeared. I think someone must have killed him." Doc coughed.

"I hear that he's back in town." He answered. "You don't know who this is, do you?"

Melvin stared and continued cutting for a few moments in silence. Then a big grin came over his face. "Man, it's been twenty five years. Where have you been hiding? What are you growing them dreads or something?" All three men laughed together. "I thought you were some bum that Pernell met in the street last night." They spent the rest of the afternoon catching up.

After the shop closed, Melvin drove Pernell and Doc home. Ruth still lived in the same house in the same neighborhood. Melvin had called before they left and told her that he had a surprise for her. He and Pernell went inside first. "Ruth, sit down and close your eyes while I go get your surprise."

"Melvin, if you brought me some rib dinners, just bring them in so we can eat."

Melvin laughed. "No, I got something better than rib dinners this time. Pernell, make sure she keeps her eyes closed." Pernell nodded.

Melvin went and got Doc who was lying down in the back seat. At least now, he looked like himself only a little older instead of like a homeless bum. Doc couldn't believe the house. Ruth had the house painted and new furniture on the porch. Inside, there she sat with her hands covering her eyes. "OK, can I open my eyes now?"

"Um huh" She opened her eyes and they shined. She gasped. "Oh my God, where?" She stood up as Doc walked towards her. He hugged her. She started to cry. She sat back down as Pernell handed her some tissues. Doc sat beside her and proceeded to tell her what had happened. As soon as he told her about the house call request she hollered, "I knew it! An angel came to me in a dream and told me that if you went on a house call that I may not see you again. When you disappeared, I went to see Esther at the House of Meditations. I told her that you had disappeared. She told me that as long as I kept your love in my heart then I would see you again. She couldn't tell me if a curse had been placed on you without having a piece of your physical being like your hair or a finger nail."

They talked late into the night. Doc couldn't believe how much living he had missed. In the back of his mind were the nagging questions like who would do this to him? Why would someone do this to him and now that he was back, would they do it again?

Ruth and Doc went to the House of Meditations the next day. "What is it dat you seek from this place?" They told Esther their story as she sat behind the counter with her sunglasses on and her yellow, green, black and red tam on her head. After hearing all that they had to say, Esther took some sticks that looked like incense from underneath the counter and burned the sticks in a clear glass block. The sticks caused a white smoke to rise to the top of the block. Esther held her face down in the white smoke and then she had Doc hold his face in the white smoke. She took off her shades and stared into his eyes. It was as if Doc was in a trance. As she looked in his eyes, she told Ruth and Doc exactly what happened on the day of his disappearance. Out loud she told them that a lawyer had a curse put on Doc. The curse was supposed to have killed him and his assailants were going to leave him in the woods to perish but the curse hadn't been strong enough which is why he went to sleep instead.

"Who?" asked Ruth.

"You know him." Esther replied.

"Nelson?" they both said.

Esther said, "Go see him and you shall get your answer. You people ere," she motioned to them both with her hands. "You been good to Esther. An eye for an eye, a tooth for a tooth. Esther take care of your troubles. Worry no more. Worry no more."

Doc called James and he invited him to come down to his office. Doc went with Ruth by his side. She wasn't going to lose him twice if she could help it. At least she had extra hair from his head if she needed to get some more help from Esther.

James met them in the lobby. On the way to his office, he gave them a tour of the building. James was a big time lawyer these days. His office was on the Executive floor. He was walking them through the partner's offices and there she was, the lady who had requested the house call that day long ago.

"Who is that?" Doc asked.

"That's Linda Kane, Nelson Kane's daughter. Let me introduce you." She was walking down the hall. "Excuse me, Linda." She turned around. When she saw Doc her mouth dropped wide open. "James, I'm sorry. I have a meeting right now." She turned and rushed off.

Doc laughed. "That's her alright."

"Let me at her." Ruth said.

"Ruth, remember what Esther said. Now just let it go."

"Yeah, I know. I just want to hurt her with my bare hands."

"Is there something that I should know?" James looked puzzled.

"So James, you're Nelson's right hand man right?"

"Pretty much, well, Linda is in charge in the event that something happens to her father and if something were to happen to her then I would be in charge."

Doc shook his head.

"If you start running things around here, give me a call. I'll help you out."

Two months later, the phone rung at Doc's house. "Doc, it's James. The strangest thing has happened, Linda and Nelson Kane have disappeared and I could use your help running the business, are you interested?"

Compromising Positions

"I think tonight Everett may pop the question," Lisa mentioned to her mother while they were cleaning up the kitchen.

"What question?" T.J. her little brother asked as he put the dirty dishes on the kitchen counter.

"Boy, what did I tell you about jumping in grown folks conversation?" Ellen Randall said to her son in an annoyed tone. T.J. clamped his lips tightly together. "Lisa, I know that you love him but there's just something about him that I don't trust."

"Mom, you worry too much," Lisa replied.
A car horn honked outside. "It's him." Lisa threw the dishtowel at T.J. and rushed to the door. "Don't wait up." Lisa yelled and slammed the door shut.

"Mama, what's the question that Everett is going to pop?" Ellen looked at her eight-year-old son and laughed. "Boy, what am I going to do with you?" She shook her head.

"Lisa thinks Everett may ask her to marry him tonight."

"No! I won't let her." T.J. stamped his feet and folded his arms across his chest. "I won't let Everett take Lisa away from me, forever."

Ellen bent down to her youngest and said "Don't worry baby. It's not going to happen."

"I hate Everett." T.J. frowned and pouted. "He always takes Lisa away from us." T.J. ran up to his room.

T.J. stayed in his room the rest of the night. He awoke in the middle of the night to hear his sister in tears saying, "Then in the room, he and a man…" she broke down and cried. "I can't believe the things that I did for him tonight." There were a few minutes of silence then she began to cry again. Finally, she said while swallowing back tears, "Then he told me that he was going to marry Diane Lawson. Their engagement party is next weekend."

In the days that followed, Lisa sank into a deep depression. She and Everett had dated for a year, which had included numerous dreams and promises. T.J. and Ellen tried to cheer her up but she acted as if they weren't even there. Ellen contacted Everett but he flat out told her there was nothing he could do to help.

One afternoon, T.J. came home to find the ambulance at his front door. Lisa had tried to kill herself. She was placed in Westin, the psychiatric facility at the edge of town. She never fully recovered. The way T.J. and Ellen saw it, Everett Whitfield had taken Lisa away from them after all. T.J. knew deep inside that Everett would get what he deserved one day for taking Lisa away from them.

Twenty years passed by. "Ladies, I would like to introduce you to our guest speaker today, professional football player, T.J. Randall," Juanita Lewis, hostess of the Women's Auxiliary Club, turned to T.J. and shook his hand as he took the floor. T.J. was tall, dark and handsome. He took one glance at the women seated in front of him and immediately his charismatic charm turned on along with the heat in the room as more than half of the women in the room sat hypnotized by his rich voice and mesmerized by his athletic build. Afterwards, as with most of his engagements, there was a long line of women that wanted his autograph and a chance to slip him their phone number.

He was preparing to leave when he felt a tap on his arm. He knew it was a female because he could smell the citrus perfume before he even turned around. "Excuse me, Mr. Randall or shall I call you, T.J.?" Standing in front of him was the perfect Georgia peach, he thought to himself, southern accent and all. He should know because he was from Georgia himself. She was light-skinned and petite with perfectly manicured hair and nails. She was in excellent condition for a middle-aged woman.

"T.J.'s the name and your name is?" He knew instantly who she was.

"Diane Whitfield." She drawled as she edged closer to him.

"Diane, I'm pleased to meet you."

She touched his hand. "I came over to get an autograph for my son. He just adores you," she said as she patted her chest as if she were clearing her throat while sizing him up. And so do you, T.J. thought to himself.

"I'd like to get your number," she stated staring into his eyes. "My husband, Everett Whitfield, president of the First Community Bank could use your help in promoting the business. Not to mention I have some other activities that might interest you."

"Such as?" he questioned. She flashed a smile and said, "I thought that I might be able to interest you in some extra curricular activities."

Just like I thought, he said to himself. She's falling all over my lap. "Let me get your number," he suggested. "I'll have my publicist give you a call to set something up."

She touched his hand. "I would really appreciate it if we could talk...maybe over dinner. How about Monday night at say 7:30?" She slipped a piece of paper into the palm of his hand and walked away.

T.J. breathed deeply as he threw his suit jacket into the back of his convertible Benz. So much for another day at the office, he thought. He couldn't believe that Diane Whitfield had dropped in his lap. He sat in the car and loosened his tie. He knew what he had to do. He picked up his cell phone. "Paige, its T.J., find out as much as you can on Everett and Diane Whitfield within the next 24 hours."

When T.J. pulled up to the Whitfield house on Monday night, it looked like no one was home. However he knew that wasn't the case. He rang the doorbell. Diane came to the door breathless. "I've been expecting you." She led him to the dining room where a full course meal was spread out on the table. "I apologize but my husband is away on business."

I know. T.J. thought.

"The maid prepared this before she left." She waved her hand toward the table. She clapped her hands and soft contemporary jazz began to play. "Are you hungry?"

"Hmm!" T.J. looked at her dressed in a transparent leopard skin jumpsuit, which revealed a black teddy underneath.

"Would you care to dance instead?" She was standing so close to him that he could smell the alcohol on her breath. She started to dance slowly in front of him as if she were a harem girl. He grabbed her around the waist and pulled her towards him.

She swayed her hips into him and wrapped her arms around him. He was immediately surrounded by her citrus scent. She looked up at him. "I could tell that you were an excellent dancer among other things." With that comment, she proceeded to grind her hips deeper into his body. He felt himself beginning to give in a little too much as he grabbed her behind. Their lips met slowly as they continued to glide right along with the music, dancing as if they were one. He was just about to pick her up and carry her to the sofa when the phone rang. "The machine will pick it up," she murmured.

Just then the voice came over the machine. "I'm calling for Mr. T.J. Randall. Please tell him there's an urgent message." T.J. grabbed the phone.

"I'm sorry, Diane, but I must leave. I have some business that I must take care of immediately."

"Can't it wait a while longer?" she looked disturbed.

"No, I'm sorry it can't. Can we reschedule our meeting?" He walked over and kissed her long and hard on the lips as she grinded her hips into him. When they finally came up for air, he told her that he wouldn't take no for an answer.

"Neither will I," she whispered.

"I'll be out of town for a couple of days but call my service and leave a message letting me know when you will be available."

Diane left a message less than 24 hours later that she wanted to reschedule their meeting for midday when he got back in town.

Everett couldn't believe his luck. The stripper on his arm was gorgeous. They walked arm in arm to the private rooms in the back. He was so excited that he could hardly contain himself. She noticed his excitement. She placed her hand on his crotch while they were walking. "We don't have to go in there you know," she said as she felt his excitement increase in her hand.

"But my friend is waiting," Everett said in a low tone.

"We can do a little something out here first if you want." The stripper smiled. He pulled her arm along to the room.

"Welcome to the ground breaking ceremony for the new site of the Elmwood First Community Bank branch." T.J. stood in the crowd and watched as Everett dug the first hole at the new site with Diane smiling by his side. T.J.'s stomach started to get queasy as memories of his sister's pain over this jerk rushed back to him.

After the ceremony, T.J. walked over to Diane and Everett. "Oh!" Diane shrieked. She was definitely surprised to say the least when she saw T.J. "Everett, I want you to meet T? Uh? T?"

"T.J. Randall," T.J. said as he held out his hand.

"T.J. plays professional football for the Dolphins."

"Is that right?" Everett stared at him hard as he shook his hand. "You look familiar. Have we met before?" Everett looked at him still searching for the answer. "Uh, TV maybe?" T.J. smiled and pointed his finger at him.

"Yeah," Everett said as he relaxed his look. "That's probably it. I don't look at much football. I haven't had much time but that's probably where I've seen you."

"I told T.J. that you might be interested in having him promote the bank," Diane said.

"That's a great idea." Everett nodded. "Here's my card, give me a call and my secretary can set something up." Just then Everett was pulled away. Diane and T.J. were left alone. "What are you doing here? Didn't you get my message?"

"Yeah, but I couldn't wait that long. I had to see you."

"I can stop by your place later this afternoon," she said.

"I'm busy this afternoon but come to my place tomorrow."

"I can't wait," she said as she stared her prize possession up and down before she walked away.

Diane appeared like clockwork. The maid let her in and showed her to the pool where T.J. was doing his daily laps. She melted in her seat by the pool as she watched him flex the rippling muscles in his upper body and thighs. He caught her staring at him. "Do you like what you see?"

"Umm, very much."

"Why don't you join me? I have some suits that you may be able to fit." He showed her the range of suits that he had for her to choose from.

"I take it you do this often." She laughed.

"Well, I never know who may stop by." He winked and turned to leave but she insisted that he stay and tell her which suit he liked. They never made it back to the pool. Once he saw the first bathing suit on her, his body told her right away that swimming was not on his mind. He kissed her face and neck and slowly proceeded to slip the straps of the bathing suit off her shoulders. Once he had removed the suit entirely, he wrapped her up in a beach towel and carried her to his bedroom.

There he laid her on his bed and began kissing her starting at her forehead working his way down. By the time, he got to her belly button; she could take no more. She grabbed his cheeks as he looked up at her. She wiggled underneath him. She felt like she was on fire, as did he. Once their bodies intertwined, they quickly reached the point of no return. Afterwards, she confided in him that she and Everett hadn't slept together in quite sometime.

Once they got up she began looking at the photos that he had throughout the house. She picked up one of Lisa and asked, "Who is this?"

"Why?" he asked.

"She looks familiar to me," she said as he could see her searching her mind.

"Oh," he quickly took the picture out of her hands and sat it down. "She's one of my relatives who lives out of town. I don't think that you know her." Diane shrugged and continued looking at the other photos.

From that day forward, Diane wanted to be with T.J. every available moment. However, that was not exactly what T.J. had in mind and he dealt with her accordingly. He did meet with Everett and filmed a commercial for the First Community Bank. Everett told T.J. that he was going to show a preview of the commercial at his next board of directors meeting and that he would like T.J. to attend, if possible. T.J. thought that it was an excellent idea. After making plans with

Everett, he called Diane and set up a rendezvous with her at her house the afternoon of the board meeting.

"And now ladies and gentlemen, please direct your attention to the monitor at the front of the room for a preview of our new campaign ad."

T.J. was sitting next to Everett. The video began with T.J. walking towards the screen with a football in his hand and football players practicing in the background. "When I think about my financial future, I think about….," the video immediately switched to Everett on all fours naked on leopard skin satin sheets in a red lit room. The stripper was kneeling down on the bed kissing him. His male friend was riding him from behind. People in the room gasped and started whispering to each other. Everett sat silently gripping the sides of the table. Beads of sweat were forming on his forehead. He didn't even notice T.J. get up and leave while the video was still playing.

He headed right over to Everett's house to see Diane. That particular afternoon, they started off with some small talk and a couple of cocktails. Before they finished their first drink, he had her stretched out on the bed blindfolded giving her a body massage. He reached for his handcuffs.

Everett noticed that the front door was cracked open when he went to put his key in the door. He peeked through the crack in the door. "Diane?" The house was silent except for the loud high-pitched quick moans coming from his bedroom. "Diane?" he said louder. The noises continued as he walked towards his bedroom door.

"What the hell is going on?" Everett announced standing in the middle of his bedroom looking down at Diane blindfolded, moaning through the tape covering her mouth and handcuffed to the bed with a handkerchief in her mouth.

When he removed the blindfold, she had a crazy look in her eyes. He pulled the tape from her mouth. She took several deep breaths. She motioned to the nightstand where there was a small key. He unlocked her hands from the bedposts. "I was molested!" she hollered.

"What?" he couldn't believe all the events that were happening to him that day. She got up and walked over to the T.V. where there was a note on the screen that said to turn on the video. Everett walked up behind her and pulled the yellow post-it note off of her back.

He held it up in front of her face. It read, "How come your wife doesn't make love to you like she does to me? If she did then you wouldn't have a secret, now would you?" Just then, she hit the play button on the VCR. The same commercial started to come on that played earlier at the bank. After Diane saw Everett's rendezvous, she slapped him. "Oh my god, I thought I was the only one you tried that with. What are you some kind of freak?"

"Get out!" she screamed as she started to cry. Everett hesitated for a second however he thought it best to leave since she had no idea about the other half of his day which had been just as bad. He had been fired. Everett walked out of the door.

My work here is done. T.J. thought to himself as he watched Everett leave the house and get in his car. To think that he had my sister do the same things that were happening on that video the night that she thought that they were going to be engaged. He let out a sigh. Some people never change.

For Better or Worse

"Mr. Tingle, I want to buy that TV over there," Clem Watson loudly announced in Tingle's TV store. The year was 1947. TVs were a luxury to have in the household. However, here was Clem Watson the only black man in the entire store saying that he wanted to purchase the most expensive TV in the store all because his wife, Pearl, wanted one.

Mr. Tingle smiled at Clem. "Now boy, how much money you got to spend on a TV?" They had an audience at the front counter.

"That depends. How much did you say it was?" There were giggles from the crowd.

"Boy, you trying to get smart with me?" Mr. Tingle looked at Clem sternly.

"Uh, no sir not at all. I just want to know how much for the TV. Then I'll be on my way."

Mr. Tingle nodded and said, "Well, this RCA is top of the line. It cost two hundred dollars."

"Two hundred huh?" Clem repeated as Mr. Tingle nodded his head. "I'll, I'll," Clem stuttered when he got nervous. "I'll be back to get it Saturday morning." The crowd started buzzing.

"Boy, you making fun up in here?" The crowd got quiet. Tingle peeked down at Clem through the top of his bifocals.

"I said I'll be back Saturday to pick it up," Clem huffed and turned to leave.

"Boy, if you playing don't bother coming back cause I'll have Sheriff Stanley waiting for you. Now, git before I call him on you for causing a scene in my store." Clem walked out calmly. He knew what he needed to do.

Clem wasn't a rich man not by any means. However, he was a very hard worker. He would go without lunch to buy something to please Pearl. You may ask why and the answer is quite simple. Pearl was Clem's one and only love. She was smart, at least smarter than he was about most things. She knew this and yet she didn't treat him like a child nor was she mean and nasty to him. She was very patient with him. She knew this was necessary in order to get the things that she wanted and she didn't mind because Clem was very obedient when it came to her wants and needs. She cooked, cleaned, bore his children and quietly educated him when needed on being a father and the head of his household.

That Friday night Clem went over to the town of Ellabelle to Smitty's. The jook joint was jumping. He walked to the back to the last booth and sat down facing the wall. Everyone else was on the floor dancing. No one was sitting down. In seconds, Runion appeared and sat across from him.

As Clem knew that he would. You see everyone in Ellabelle knew about Runion. Quiet as it was kept people called Runion the devil's brother behind his back. No one dare call him that to his face for fear of a deathly curse or death. Runion could provide anything you wanted for a price, normally, a very unearthly high price. No one knew exactly when Runion first showed up in town however, the oldest people in town remember Runion from their youthful days and word had it that he had never in his life looked a day past 45 years old. "How much money you need?" Runion asked. Clem raised his brows.

"A lot," he said.

Runion nodded his head. "You can have an unlimited supply of cash but it'll cost you."

"I'm good for it just let me know what I owe you." Clem said. Runion let out a hollow laugh that could wake up the dead. People dancing nearby moved out of the way.

"Oh, oh, he's got another poor soul," a few mumbled as they sadly shook their heads while hustling to another corner in the joint as if a fight were about to break out.

"I get your soul at 5 p.m., eighteen thousand and eighty days from now," Runion stated using his long pinky fingernail to pick his black rotted teeth.

Clem looked blank. "What day is that?" he asked.

"Why that's, March 12th, 1998," Runion replied without hesitating.

Clem didn't even blink twice. He looked at Runion and said, "You got a deal."

Runion continued digging deeper into his rotten teeth. "If you try to kill yourself, I'll just get you sooner." He grinned. Clem was sitting in Tingle's doorway when he came to open up his store on Saturday morning.

"What can I do you for boy?" Tingle said suspiciously.

"I'm here for the TV," Clem stood up and brushed off the back of his pants.

"You got the money?"

Clem shook his head.

Once inside, Tingle ran to the back of the store and made a telephone call. "Stanley, I need to see you over at the store right away. It's urgent. This will interest you." He came back out front slowly. "Boy, it's going to take me a few minutes to get the TV. Make yourself comfortable, while I finish opening up. Then I'll be with you." Clem nodded and leaned against the countertop as he waited. As Sheriff Stanley was getting out of the car, Tingle proceeded to get the TV out of the back of the store. He had the TV at the front of the store as the sheriff entered. "That'll be two hundred dollars." Clem took the wad of bills out of his pocket and counted out two hundred dollars.

"That's a lot of money, you got there boy," Sheriff Stanley said. Clem just nodded his head and put the remaining bills back in his pocket.

"That your lifesaving's there, ain't it boy?" the sheriff asked. Clem picked up the TV and walked to the door. "Boy, you hear me talking to you?" The sheriff said louder.

"It's, its just some money that I have," Clem said slowly. Then he walked out of the store. He placed the TV on his backseat. As he turned around the sheriff was standing right in front of him.

"Look boy, I don't know what you're up to but you better hope that I don't find out that you're doing something wrong in the eyes of the law."

Clem nodded and said, "Yes Sir" as he proceeded to get in his car and drive off with the sheriff watching his every move. As time went by, Sheriff Stanley would always manage to appear when any merchandise was being picked up or delivered for Clem and Pearl. When Clem brought his first brand new Cadillac, the sheriff served them with a search warrant. He placed Clem in the holding cell while he conducted a search of the house.

"Boy, I don't understand how you can afford these things but I'm going to keep watching you 'til I find out," Sheriff Stanley drawled.

Clem let out a heavy sigh. "If you want to know go to Ellabelle and see a guy by the name of Runion."

The sheriff nodded and said, "I just might do that." Sheriff Stanley let Clem go since he couldn't find any evidence of any wrongdoing. Clem had a dream that night that he went back to Smitty's. There he saw Sheriff Stanley meeting with Runion. Runion let out a mean nasty laugh that scared Clem. The sheriff laughed as well. Clem knew instantly that Runion didn't like the sheriff at all. Yet Runion went with the sheriff out to his car. Clem saw them driving down the road. Runion was picking his teeth with his dirty fingernails. Then he proceeded to stick his pinky nail, which was suddenly as sharp as a small knife into the sheriff's neck. Clem woke up instantly. It was pitch black in the middle of the night. He knew that Sheriff Stanley was dead.

They found the sheriff's car at the bottom of a hill all burnt up. From the looks of it, people assumed that he had fallen asleep while driving and ran off the road. But those that saw Sheriff Stanley at Smitty's with Runion that night knew exactly what had happened. However, they knew better than to tell the law or anyone else for that matter. Clem's conscious began to bother him about what Runion had done to Sheriff Stanley. Pearl noticed a change in Clem's demeanor so she asked him what was troubling him. Clem blurted out the deal with Runion without going into the morbid deals. He told her only that the payback would be made in time. Pearl had a funny look in her eyes by the time he finished telling her about the deal.

"You lucky soul, we're rich!" She let out a haunting laugh and hugged him. Pearl immediately wanted a new house built with all new appliances, a closet full of new clothes and a new car. From then on, every year everyone in the house had to have a new car, a new wardrobe and a vacation of their choice. One of the good uses of their new fortune was that they were able to send their children away to get a college education. However, with the kids gone, Clem began to regret telling Pearl about Runion more than telling Sheriff Stanley. He watched Pearl change before his eyes from an intelligent, loving patient woman into a lazy, greedy, mindless blob. She quit her job and began spending all of her time in front of the TV. The next thing Clem knew she weighed over 300 pounds. She began barking out orders to him, to buy her more things or to get up and get things for her around the house, instead of having just a plain old conversation with him like she used to do. Clem on the other hand kept his job. He enjoyed his job and his co-workers. He brought things for himself every now and then but not in excess. The children returned home to visit periodically however, it disturbed them to see their mother sit at home wasting away as a mindless blob. After graduating, they set up their homes elsewhere in the world.

The years passed and Pearl's weight finally got the best of her and she had a stroke. It was determined that it was best if she were moved into a nursing home. Without her around the house, Clem became lonely very quickly and soon began to deteriorate mentally and physically. His children weren't able to care for him as they had busy lives of their own so they did the only thing that they could think of to make him happy. They put him in the nursing home with Pearl that was a beautiful facility considering they were financially able to afford one of the best nursing homes in the area. Happy he was indeed for he still loved his wife, Pearl.

He was the healthiest person actually living at the nursing home. Mentally he was a little forgetful at times about where he left his reading glasses. Physically, he moved around a little slower but so did everyone else his age. Clem helped the staff at the Edgewood Rest Home move the patients around, feed them, you name it. He helped so much that most patients' families thought that he was part of the staff. Clem loved helping out. It made him feel useful. Plus, it kept him busy. The patients and staff became very attached to him. Pearl on the other hand spent her days fussing and cussing at Clem and the staff to get them to wait on her every want and need. She had grown accustomed to this treatment at home and it didn't seem to make sense to her that she should rehabilitate herself by doing things for herself instead of relying on others. Clem knew that Pearl lost her mind the day that he told her about the deal with Runion. Some days, he cried because he missed his wife.

"Nurse Jenkins, did you bring the paper to me today?" Clem asked.

"Sure did. Here you go." She handed him the paper across the counter at the nurse's station. Clem took the paper out on the front porch and sat down by Walt.

"Walt, I got the paper," he said loudly. Walt was going deaf and couldn't read so Clem would read the paper to him everyday. Walt nodded. "The Mets beat the Yankees 5-0."

"They did?" Walt responded. "Now that's one for the books." He smiled. "What's today's date?" he asked.

"Uh, let's see. Today is, oh my goodness. Today is March 12th 1998," Clem said the last sentence slowly.

"Year's going fast. I can't believe it's March already," Walt said watching the cars drive down the street.

"You can say that again," Clem said solemnly. "Walt, I'm gonna die today."

"Whatcha say? Speak up, I can't hear you." Walt said louder as if Clem was the one who had the hearing problem.

Clem pulled his chair closer. "I said I'm gonna die at 5 p.m."

Walt laughed. "What do you mean you wanna pie at 5 p.m.? You gotta eat your supper first."

Clem held up his hand. "Wait!" He went inside to get a pen. He wrote it on a piece of paper and showed it to Walt.

"Oh! Man, you're healthy as a horse. Stop exaggerating." Walt laughed to himself.

Clem went inside. "Nurse Jenkins" Clem stated as he held out his hand. She didn't know how to respond. He took her hand and shook it as he said, "It's been a pleasure."

"Clem, you going somewhere? Are your kids here to pick you up?"

He looked at her and said, "I'll be gone by 5 p.m."

"Ok, well I'll see you when you get back," she remarked.

After what he had gone through on the porch with Walt, he didn't bother explaining the details to her. And so it went that morning.

He told Pearl that he would be gone by 5 p.m. and she looked at him with a blank look on her face and said, "Buy me some new pajamas while you're out."

By lunchtime, he had said goodbye to everyone in the place. By coincidence for lunch, they had his favorite meal, fried fish and cabbage. Normally after lunch, he took a nap but he knew that he didn't have long. He called his daughter, Joyce and his son, Stanley.

Then he called his best friend, Fred. "Fred, I need you to do me a favor. Can you come take me to run a couple of errands this afternoon?" Fred was there in about forty-five minutes. It was one o'clock. The first place they went was to the baseball field. There was a doubleheader game going on. He and Fred sat by the catcher's mound drinking and talking about old times. They left during the fifth inning. It was 3:30 and Clem had another stop to make before five o'clock. They went to Miss Lucy's. He wanted to dance with a woman once more. He picked the closest woman that he could find that reminded him of a young Pearl. He danced and danced thinking about Pearl all the while until he felt a sharp pain that knocked him off his feet. Fred bent over him.

"What's wrong, Clem?"

"What time is it?" Clem asked barely above a whisper.

"Uh, it's 4:30," Fred answered.

"Take me home," Clem whispered.

Fred got Clem back to Edgewood. They put him in his bed. All the while, he had a smile on his face with his eyes closed humming to himself.

"Whatcha thinking about?" Fred asked him.

"I'll talk at you later. I'm dancing with my girl Pearl right now."

Meantime, his wife Pearl was hollering across the room at Clem. "Where are my pajama's you old fool?" Everyone ignored her and continued to care for Clem. Finally, she hollered "I sure do wish I had your lucky soul over here, Clem. At least, I would get some attention."

A few seconds later, Clem sat up with his eyes wide open. "Runion!" he said surprised and then he glanced over to see Pearl slumped over dead. The clock on their room wall said five o'clock on the dot.

Family Trait

"Hi Grandpa!" Cameron gave Avery a peck on the cheek and ran into the house.

"Hi Pops," Trey said slowly while he strolled over to the porch furniture. He slouched down into a chair. The car horn honked as the children's mother waved and drove off.

"What's the matter son? Sounds like you got something on your mind." Avery asked concerned. Trey didn't say anything. "Trey, what's wrong?"

"You won't laugh at me will you?" Avery glanced over at Trey sideways. He could see that something was bothering him.

"Naw, I won't laugh."

"Grandpa, you ever liked a girl and you weren't sure if she really liked you or if she was just playing with you."

Avery chuckled. "I ain't laughing at you, son. I'm laughing at women and the predicaments that they can get us men into. Women can be complicated but don't let their actions confuse you. They are really sensitive creatures and all they want is love. Always! Tell me about this girl. I might be able to help you figure this out." Avery pulled a cigar out of his shirt pocket and lit it. Trey sat up and leaned towards Avery.

"Her name is Jessica and she goes to my school. We eat lunch together everyday with a group of other friends and the more that I talked to her, the more we became friends. I've met her at the mall a couple of times and we went to the movies once. Every time we've met outside of school, she spends more time talking with her friends than to me." Avery smiled.

"Trey, what grade are you in now?"

"9th grade."

"So your parents are bringing you to the mall or the movies to meet this girl?"

"Yeah, me and my friends will meet her and her friends there."

"Have you ever thought that she's doing this cause she's nervous around you?"

"But how come she's not nervous when we talk at school?" Trey said in a frustrated tone.

"You're with a group at school. When you're at the movies, you're talking to her one on one, right?" Avery looked over at Trey out of the corner of his eyes. Trey had his fingers under his chin. He broke out in a smile and nodded.

"Listen here, when I was about your age, I had my first crush on a girl. I didn't tell anybody about it but my momma knew. She probably figured it out cause I suddenly took an interest in my appearance and I cared more about the clothes that I wore. Anyhow, she knew and she sat me down and she told me that all women really want is love. Even if they act funny and treat you bad. All they want is love it's just sometimes they are looking for love from the wrong fellow and not you or they are looking for love from you but they are either too nervous to tell you or they don't know how to tell you. All you can do in those situations is be kind to them, be patient, a gentleman always and see what happens."

"The first gal that I felt like that about was Irene Williams. We were in the same 9th grade class and she always dressed nice and smelled good. She started coming over my house to see your Aunt Cynthia. We would laugh and talk when she would come over. I thought she was coming over cause she liked me and she was just using visiting Aunt Cynthia as an excuse but when I asked her to the homecoming dance, she flat out told me no with a frown on her face. Then I got angry and I asked her point blank why she was looking at me like that and I said it with a frown on my face. She said that she didn't mean to say it like that. She told me that she liked William Johnson. He was a Junior at our high school. He was in Aunt Cynthia's class. She had been sending him notes through Aunt Cynthia. They were going to the homecoming dance together with Aunt Cynthia and her boyfriend. I was hurt to say the least and I tried to play it cool but my mother saw right through me."

"My mother talked to me again and this time she told me to be kind, patient and just enjoy life. She said that the right one would come along when I was least expecting it. Then she told me the family secret. She told me that the men in our family have a kind of sixth sense about who their spouse would be before they really know the person. She said that I would know the girl that would be my wife at first sight. I couldn't understand that and I asked her how I would know? She told me that I would know cause my wife would have an extraordinary look in my mind's eyes only. I asked her how she knew this and she told me that the same thing had happened when her parents first met."

"My grandfather, John Brooks, met my grandmother at a church picnic. It was the kick-off of their church summer revival series. It was a Sunday afternoon. Grandpa said that the food looked and smelled so good that his stomach growled before he took his first bite. His mouth watered for the golden brown fried chicken breasts."

"He was oblivious to the women serving the food until he heard this small musical voice say 'Excuse me Sir, would you like a breast?' He turned to the voice and standing behind the chicken was this petite vision that had fireworks flying over her head. It took him totally off guard and he almost dropped his plate but he caught it just in time. He was so stunned that he had to set his plate down and wipe his forehead. He thought that the heat was getting to him."

"Yes, yes Ma'am. Please." He held out his plate for the chicken, but before he moved on to the next dish, he said, "May I ask your name?"

She blushed. "Eleanor."

He bowed and said, "Ma'am, I don't mean to embarrass you or your family, but you are a vision of loveliness."

"Why, thank you." She beamed.

"May I ask you another question? Are you taken?" She shook her head no. "Would you eat with me after you're done serving?"

"I would love to," she replied. "As arranged, when Eleanor was done helping with the food, she came over and sat with John. She seemed to be very hungry. She kept her fork in her mouth most of the time. She didn't have much to say. John didn't get upset. He was stunned by her beauty and he just took her silence as she was hungry."

"Would you like to go for a walk after eating that big meal?"

She said "I can't, I have to help clean up."

"Oh, so you're staying for the service? I hear the preacher is good."

She shook her head yes and jumped up and held out her hand awkwardly and said, "Thank you for sitting with me."

"Why my pleasure." He shook her hand. "Save me a seat at the service." She rushed off before he could finish his sentence. He saw her at the service and she had a empty chair next to her. She looked at him and smiled and he nodded towards the empty chair asking if he could sit down. Before she responded a big fat woman plopped right in the empty chair next to her. After the service, he looked for her to walk her home. He spotted her in the crowd. He couldn't help but spot her since all he had to do was look for the fireworks over her head. He was on one side of the tent and she was on the other side. He tried to inch close to her and at one point she saw him but she seemed to quickly turn her head. He called out her name but she never acknowledged him. "What is with this girl? I know she saw me," he thought. The next night, he got to the revival service early. He put his bible in the empty chair next to him. He saw the fireworks before he saw her and there she was—a petite vision. He waved and she smiled. He pointed to the empty chair and she walked to another chair without a response.

He got up and walked over. "May I?" He nodded to the empty chair.

"Mr. Brooks, you need to talk to my father," she whispered in a low voice.

"Ma'am forgive my manners. Where can I find your father?" She nodded at the pulpit. The guest preacher was her father, Reverend Scott. Now he knew why he had never seen her before. He waited until after the service and he introduced himself to the preacher. He told him that he would like to court his daughter. He knew that may be a strange request since they were visiting but he was taken with his daughter's beauty. He told the Reverend what he did for a living. He ran his own farm and he let him know that the minister here at his home church could vouch for him as a person. Once the formalities were out in the open, Reverend Scott called Eleanor over. He asked Eleanor if she would like to see Mr. Brooks while they were in town.

"Yes," she smiled. That was the beginning of their courtship and they were married within the year. After hearing my grandfather's plight, I got over my first crush, Irene quickly. I knew that one day I would know who my wife would be. If I remember correctly, not long after that homecoming dance, William Johnson ended up dumping old Irene and before Christmas she started showing an interest in me again but by then I was popular with plenty girls after having a good football season so I didn't want to be tied down with her.

When I went off to Hampton Institute, I had a roommate by the name of Robert Ellis. We got along real well and we were roommates the entire time that we were at Hampton. Robert would tell me about his family but I didn't know what they looked like until we graduated. Robert's family gave him a big graduation party and I went. Robert's people had money. A bunch of us were talking in his backyard and I went into the house to get something to drink. Across the dining room table was this group of girls laughing and talking. I glanced over at the girls and there was one girl in the group that had what looked like a halo around her head. I blinked and this light stayed around her head. None of the other girls had what looked like a light around their head. The girl with the halo left the group of girls and walked over to me.

She said "Hi, I'm Odessa." She held out her hand for an introduction. When she spoke it was like music to my ears. She looked like a beautiful angel. I was so stunned by her beauty that all I could do was stare at her. "Your name is?"

"Miss I do apologize. You see I've never been in the presence of an angel before until you walked up to me and began talking with that beautiful voice of yours." She just laughed. "My name is Avery. Avery Brooks. It is my pleasure to meet you." I bowed. I was so awestruck.

"Please Mr. Brooks. You are embarrassing me." I had her friends' attention by this point. "Everyone, I would like to introduce Mr. Avery Brooks."

"It is my pleasure to be in this room full of lovely ladies." They all giggled. I had the rooms' full attention. "Mr. Brooks, where are you from?" Before I could answer, Robert walked in the room.

"There you are Avery. I should have known you would be entertaining the ladies. Odessa, I see you've met my roommate Avery." Her mouth opened in surprise.

"Oh my goodness, this is Avery; the one that you've told us about. Mr. Brooks, it's my pleasure indeed." I noticed the impressed look on her face.

"Ladies, the music is about to start playing. I'm sure that you'll want to freshen up before the dancing starts. Avery and I will see you out there on the floor."

"Ladies," I bowed out of the room. As soon as we left the room, I said, "Robert, what did you tell your sister about me?"

"Nothing. Just that you were a fine man," I just nodded and smiled. During the dance, I followed Odessa's every move and it wasn't hard to do cause in my eyes, her halo lit up the room. When I saw her go out on the dance floor, I was tapping her dance partner on the shoulder within a minute so that I could be near her. It was a slow song playing and when I grabbed her hand, I felt a ring. My heart sunk.

"Ah," I was speechless, all I could do was breathe out of my mouth. Then I looked in her face. She was a vision. "Ah" I turned my head and coughed to play it off. "Are you engaged?" She smiled.

"Yes, I am. How did you know?"

I played with her, "Why I just knew that a vision like you must have captured some man's attention." I smiled at her but deep down inside my heart was broken. "Where is the lucky fellow?" I glanced around but I didn't really want to see him. She looked around.

"Why he isn't in here," she frowned.

"Was it the fellow that you were just dancing with?"

"Why no."

"Oh, so he doesn't mind you dancing with others?" I raised my eyebrows and glanced over at her. She laughed.

"He can't dictate who I dance with," She said adamantly.

"Oh, so you're one of those headstrong women, huh?" She opened her mouth to come back with a comment but she looked at the look on my face." I looked like a lost puppy dog. She raised her eyebrows.

"Would you let your girlfriend dance with whomever she wanted?"

"Well, I might but I would be watching every man that she danced with to make sure that those fellows didn't get out of line."

Just then I felt this slap on my shoulder. I turned around and this drunk fellow said, "I need to cut in."

"Why here he is right now. Gordon, I want to introduce you to Mr. Avery Brooks. He was Robert's roommate at Hampton." Gordon nodded and turned to grab Odessa's hand to dance but he missed her hand and he swayed to hard and fell to the floor. Everyone stopped dancing. Odessa was so embarrassed at the attention that she ran out of the room. I ran after her. Gordon was too drunk to do anything. She ran outside and sat on a bench in the yard. I followed and sat right beside her. She didn't realize that I was following her and immediately put her face into her hands. She heard me sit down and when she lifted her head, she had tears rolling down her eyes. "Oh, I'm so sorry."

"Please don't apologize for that mishap back there." I handed her my handkerchief. She wiped those big pretty eyes. "May I ask you a question? You don't have to answer and please don't take offense to the question. Why are you with him?" She looked off into the dark.

"On paper, our family credentials make us appear as the perfect couple. However, in real life, Gordon is a playboy and an alcoholic. I knew this when we dated but he wined and dined me. He bought me things. We had fun together but that was back when there were no strings attached. I saw his flaws then but I thought that things would change once we became engaged. I thought that I could change him but the more that I try, the more he resists and the more frustrated I get." I shook my head. "His father is a doctor and his family wants him to become one. However, that's not what he wants to do but he doesn't know how to tell them that. So he feels trapped and he's doing everything that he can to get out of it without telling his parents to their face that he doesn't want to be a doctor. He knows that they will be crushed and he doesn't want to hurt them."

"But he's hurting you in the process."

"I'm starting to see that I'm a part of his family's idea of his perfect life but I'm not a part of his picture of the future." Her voice cracked.

"Let's go for a walk." We walked in silence for awhile. It is a beautiful night. The sky was so clear that it looked like you could reach out and touch the stars.

Finally I said "I have to tell you something. You are a beautiful woman. I just want you to know that and you don't have to go through with this marriage. I'll talk to Robert and your parents if you think that will help." She stopped and turned to me.

"Mr. Brooks."

"Please call me Avery." She had a beautiful smile on her face.

"That is such a kind thing to say. You know, my brother was right about you. You are a fine man. Thank you for walking with me." She hugged me. I couldn't leave it at that.

"Odessa, I know that you have a lot on your mind. However, I will continue to be in touch with your brother. If things don't work out with you and Gordon, I would like to take you out." She just nodded and smiled and we continued to walk in silence. As her house came into view, she stopped again and she looked into my eyes. She gave me a kiss on the cheek and thanked me for walking with her. When we got to the porch, Robert and some of the other fellows were sitting on the porch smoking. She walked into the house and I stayed outside with the fellows. Now most guys don't talk to other guys when they like your sister. That's why I laid my cards out to Odessa and not Robert. We were buddies but I know how brothers can be especially about little sisters. They are protective. Now I was respectable as his roommate but dating his sister put us in a different light. He knew how I had treated some of the girls at Hampton that I had dated. I didn't need that added stress held over my head. I went home later that night not saying a word about my conversation with Odessa to Robert. However, two weeks later, I had a birthday party and I invited Robert and told him to tell Odessa to come and bring some of her friends. She came with a couple of girlfriends.

I asked her to dance. "So how are things going?" I grabbed her hand to go out on the floor. The ring was gone and she was smiling and shaking her hips to the beat. We began dating that night. We were married within a year of my birthday. As a matter of fact, we got married on my birthday the following year.

"Did the halo go away?" Avery laughed.

"I got used to it and now I see it every now and then but I think cause I'm so used to it that I don't even see it anymore unless I look real hard." Trey's eyes were big in amazement.

"Does Grandma know?"

"I told her. She laughed like I was joking. Even to this day she laughs but I'm telling you the truth. God sent that angel, your Grandma to me." Trey smiled as did Avery.

"What happened to Grandma's boyfriend, Gordon?" Avery shook his head.

"Even though your Grandmother saw him for what he was and she let him go, he never could break away from his parents dream. He was killed in a car accident. Those that saw him last said he was drunk. So you see, he just drank himself to death."

"Did Uncle Bob accept you and Grandma dating?"

"Since we had graduated from Hampton when me and your grandmother started dating, he didn't seem to have a problem. If he did, I never heard about it. He seemed really happy for us. He was my best man at our wedding. He said at the reception that two of his favorite people in the world had gotten married that day. We lived with Grandma's family the first year we were married and then she gave birth to your daddy. After that, we needed to move cause we needed more room for your daddy to grow. We didn't have much money. I talked to my mother and she told me to ask God to provide. She said that he'll provide what you need. I knew that but I told her that I wanted to make sure that we moved to the right house in the right neighborhood."

She said "I told you when you were young how you would know that you had found your true love. The same will happen when you find the right house."

"We looked at quite a few houses. The ones that we could afford all seemed to be in bad locations, like right next to railroad tracks or across the street from the cemetery. This house came up for sale unexpectedly. Avery pointed to the porch. The family that lived here before, the father went to join his wife in the nursing home that she was in and his children wanted to sell the house quickly so they put this house on the market for a low asking price so that they could get rid of it. They apparently didn't need money. When the realtor showed us this house, I was skeptical. The neighborhood at the time was predominantly white and we would be the second black family in the neighborhood and I wasn't sure that we would be well received. I had a wife and baby. I didn't need no trouble where I had to worry about their safety. I saw the halo again when we saw this house. I knew that this was the house for us but I was more than a little anxious about moving in it. But I prayed to the good Lord. I asked him to keep us safe. With the month, Ms Sadie moved in the neighborhood and within a year most of the white folks had moved. We've got good neighbors. Ms Sadie watches the house when we're away and we do the same for her. You grew up playing with Taj down the street. Your father grew up playing with Taj's father until drugs got the best of him. Your father was about your age when we had a similar conversation as you and I are having today."

"You know your father and mother met at Hampton." Trey nodded as his Grandpa kept talking. "I remember the day that your father came home telling me about your mother. He knew that she was the one cause he had seen her face in a dream before he met her for the first time. After they got married they lived with us until they had you, Avery Joseph Brooks, III. You are my third generation namesake. Your father had a dream about the house you live in now before it even went for sale. Once the sign went up and he saw it, he knew that it was the one. Now I'm not saying that you need to dump Jessica cause we know that she's not the one. It sounds to me like she's probably shy and you maybe her first boyfriend so she's probably nervous. Just be patient with her, be kind, be a gentleman always and most important enjoy life cause you only get one. But just know that when it's time to settle down, God will send you a sign regarding the one that you will marry and where you will settle down. In the meantime, enjoy life."

"What are you two out here talking about?" Odessa came outside with Cameron following her.

"We're out here talking man business," Avery said.

"Well, do you mind if two ladies come sit out here and join you?"

"Not at all, we have just finished our conversation."

"May I ask what you were discussing?"

"Why, that's man's business."

Odessa looked at Avery and Trey with a smile on her face. "Trey?"

"Grandma, Grandpa was just telling me that there are angels walking around right here on earth right before our eyes." Odessa sat down between the two of them and patted Avery's knee.

"So you've been telling Trey about your angel, huh?"

"Oh, I like angels. Can I hear that story?" Cameron's eyes lit up.

"Come here, baby girl, that's a story that I'll share with you when you get older but let me tell you about the first angel that God ever gave me, my mother." Cameron sat on Avery's lap to hear the story.

Ms. Cindy

"Grandma! Sheeda! I'm home," Taj yelled as he swung the front door open with a loud bang. Taj threw down his bookbag in the living room and bounced into the kitchen. "Hmm, I wonder what Grandma and Sheeda are doing," he thought to himself as his stomach growled. He couldn't wait to eat his afternoon snack. He had played all morning at school. He had a substitute teacher for his fifth grade class that morning. The kitchen was empty so he kicked his shoes off and tiptoed back to the bedrooms. Sheeda, his little sister, was in her bed fast asleep. Taj frowned at the sight. "She must be sick," he thought. He proceeded back to Grandma's room.

There he saw a strange woman going through his grandma's pocketbook while his grandmother lay asleep in her bed. He caught the stranger by surprise.

"Hello baby!" The stranger jumped when she saw him staring at her. "How was school today?" Taj looked at this woman like she was crazy.

"Who are you?" he asked suspiciously. She grabbed his arm and proceeded to usher him down the hall.

The woman smiled. "Just call me Ms. Cindy."

"Ms. Cindy?" he frowned. "Grandma never told me about you before. How does she know you?"

"She's a friend of mine. Sometimes, she comes to the park with your sister and we sit and talk while your sister plays at the playground."

"Is Grandma alright?" "She's not feeling well baby. She asked me to take care of you and your sister while she gets some rest." He quickly worked his hand out of hers and headed back down the hall.

"Where are you going?"

"I'm going to get Sheeda and go to Ms. Sadie's house."

"No, no baby, you don't need to go to Ms. Sadie's house." Ms. Cindy walked toward him.

"Grandma always told me if she gets sick or in case of any emergency, we're to go to Ms. Sadie's." He turned and headed right back down the hallway.

"Henry?" She grabbed his shoulder. "Henry, this time she told me to watch you."

"My name isn't Henry." He frowned.

"Boy, you know what your name is," she said loudly as if she had lost her patience with him. He looked at her like she was crazy. She ignored his look and said "I'm sure that your Grandma probably just forgot to tell me about Ms. Sadie before she went to lie down. I'll wait here with you until she wakes up. I made some hot chocolate for you in the kitchen. Come on and have a snack while Sheeda and your Grandma get some rest." He didn't hesitate for a second. He turned and followed Ms. Cindy to the kitchen.

When he woke up, he was not in his bedroom. As he looked around the room, he realized that he was in a strange place. The room had two twin beds with a box of toys at the foot of each bed. One box had boy toys and the other box was filled with girl toys. The smell of bacon cooking filled the air. He walked across the room to open the door. He pulled on the door but it wouldn't budge. He knocked on the door. No answer. He banged on the door with his fists and shouted, "Let me out of here." A woman's voice said from the other side of the door, "I'll be with you in a few minutes."

"I gotta go to the bathroom," he hollered.

"Can you hold it for a few minutes?" He nodded his head. "Can you?" asked the voice from the other end of the door.

"Yes." He went and sat back on the bed with a truck that he grabbed from the box filled with boy toys. He finally heard the key in the lock after what felt like an eternity.

Ms. Cindy peeked her head in the door and said, "Mornin Henry!"

"I'm Taj," he let out a frustrated breath.

"Where's Sheeda?" he immediately demanded.

"Right here," Sheeda's dimpled smiling face appeared as the door opened.

" Taj!" she ran to her brother and hugged him. She was 3 years old going on 30 with a head full of curly ringlets.

"Where's Grandma and where are we?" Taj threw out the questions so fast it was as if he was playing the game show Jeopardy for real money.

Cindy laughed. "Come on professor. Go to the bathroom and come eat some breakfast before you use up all your brain cells." Sheeda grabbed his hand and pulled him towards the door.

Once he sat down at the kitchen table and began eating, Cindy answered his questions. "Henry, you live here with me, Sheila and your little brother, Rodney."

"I'm not Henry. I'm Taj and that's Sheeda." He pointed to his little sister sitting next to him eating at the table. "I don't have a brother named Rodney." he frowned.

Cindy ignored him and said, "Grandma's sick so you'll have to stay home from school today and watch Rodney." She turned and gave her baby a piece of what was bacon.

"Here you go, Rodney." Rodney held the bacon in his balled up fist.

"I gotta get ready for school." Taj's eyes got big as if he had forgotten what day it was.

"No!" she got loud again. "I told you that I need you to watch Rodney today while I go to work."

"What about Grandma?" Taj asked.

"I'll take you to see her after I get off of work if you both behave and watch Rodney until I get home."

"I don't know how to watch a baby. I never did it before." Taj's eyebrows went up.

"Henry, don't play games with me. You've watched Rodney plenty times before." Cindy said loudly and impatiently.

"He's not Henry." Sheeda yelled at Cindy.

"Sheila!" Sheeda got a shocked look on her face and she burst out crying. Taj knew something was wrong with this woman. He knew that he'd better do what she said until he could figure out how to get him and Sheeda out of there. Ms. Cindy picked Sheeda up and carried her into her bedroom. Sheeda screamed louder. "Do you want the belt?"

"No!" Sheeda screamed.

"Then be quiet!" Ms Cindy closed the bedroom door with Sheeda softly crying. She walked back into the kitchen.

"I forgot what to do for Rodney. Can you please remind me?" Taj asked quietly.

"It's real simple. I'm going to put him to sleep before I leave. When he wakes up, give him a bottle of milk from the refrigerator and his jar of baby food. Then just let him crawl on the floor until he falls asleep. I should be back before he wakes up this evening."

"When you come home, we're gonna go see Grandma, right?"

"Yeah sure," she said quickly then she grabbed Rodney and went into her bedroom to get ready for work. As promised Rodney was fast asleep when she got ready to leave.

"Here's a list of chores that I need you to do while I'm gone." She handed the list to Taj and went out the door. Sheeda was allowed to leave the bedroom and watch Blues Clues on the TV in the living room. Taj wasn't sure about all of this but he knew that he'd be alright once he saw Grandma. He looked at the list. He had enough work to do for a week. He started by washing the breakfast dishes. He saw the phone on the kitchen wall. "I can call Grandma and if she's not home, I'll call Keith," he thought. Keith was Taj's big brother through the Big Brother/Big Sister organization. Those were the only two phone numbers that he knew by heart. He picked up the phone and put the receiver to his ear as he prepared to dial. "That's funny," he thought. "There's no buzzing noise coming from the phone." He hung up the phone and picked up the receiver. He hit the dial tone button several times. The phone was broken.

He had Sheeda sweep the linoleum floor. She danced around the floor with the broom as if the broom was her Prince Charming and she was Cinderella. Afterwards, he mopped the floor. The baby woke up from his nap. Sheeda entertained the baby while Taj finished the floor.

"Let's take the baby out for a walk."

Sheeda rushed to the door. "I'm ready." She loved to go places.

"What?" Taj looked at Sheeda standing by the door. He smacked his hand to his head and shook it. "Girl, where is your coat?"

"Alright already, I'll get it." She slumped and went into Cindy's bedroom where she slept and got her coat. Taj put the snowsuit he found in the bedroom on Rodney. After they all had their coats on, Sheeda held the stroller while Taj put Rodney in it.

Taj turned the deadbolt lock and the lock in the doorknob. The door was still locked and there were no more locks to turn. He pulled on the door as hard as he could. He beat and banged on it. "Ugh!"

Sheeda pulled and banged on the door to help him. She began to cry and then the baby seeing her upset began to cry too. Taj stared at the door. There was a lock up high that didn't have a knob to turn. It had a keyhole instead. They were trapped. "I want Nana. I want Nana." Sheeda began to chant with tears rolling down her cheeks.

"We're going to see Grandma. We'll just have to wait for Cindy to take us," Taj said calmly. He took off Rodney's coat and his coat. Sheeda fell asleep with her coat on.

That afternoon, Taj sat looking out the window. They were in a high rise project on what looked like the 12th floor of a eighteen-story building from the looks of the high rise buildings surrounding them. Kids were coming from school with their backpacks and lunch boxes in hand. Hey there's Rochelle. His mind started racing. He raised the window and yelled Rochelle's name but she didn't hear him.

Officer Stanley had talked to his class about strangers that may try to lure them from their family. He thought back to yesterday. He remembered walking to the kitchen with Cindy drinking his hot chocolate and the next thing he remembered was waking up here.

"Sheeda, did Ms. Cindy come to visit Grandma yesterday?" She shook her head up and down and kept on watching the TV show "Hey Arnold" which had her full attention. "Did she give you something to drink?" No answer. Taj turned off the T.V. Sheeda got up and pushed him.

"Stop it, turn on the T.V." She grabbed at him as he held the remote over his head.

"Listen Sheeda, I need to ask you something. It's important. Once you answer, I'll turn the T.V. back on."

"What!" She rolled her eyes and pulled at her hair.

"Did Ms. Cindy give you something to drink at home yesterday?"

"Yes" She rolled her eyes again.

"Did you go to sleep after that?" Same response. "Did you see her give Grandma anything to drink?"

"No, I was watching T.V."

"What were they doing while you were watching T.V.?" She shrugged her shoulders. "Listen, Sheeda put on your thinking cap for me and think real hard about what you remember them doing." Sheeda put on her invisible thinking cap.

"Um," she put her forefinger to her lips. "Ms. Cindy and Nana went into Nana's room."

"Good girl. Now you can watch T.V." Taj noticed a picture of a boy and girl on top of the T.V. I bet that's Henry and Sheila. Taj thought to himself. Henry was around his age and Sheila looked a little older than Sheeda.

"Let's go see my Grandma now." Cindy had just come in the front door. Taj picked up his coat and put it on.

"Wait a minute, I just got in here."

"You said this morning that we would go see Grandma when you got home."

"Yeah, let me get in the door first. Now just you sit your tail down," Cindy said angrily. Taj wasn't surprised but he knew that he needed to stay alert for the rest of the evening.

As soon as Taj finished the dinner dishes, "Can we go to Grandma's house now?" he asked.

"No" she said quick and nasty. They sat and watched T.V.

"Who is that?" He pointed to the pictures on top of the T.V.

"You know that you and Sheila." He just stared at the picture and didn't say a word.

"Can Sheeda please sleep with me tonight?"

"Sure, that girl kicked me half the night."

"Can we camp out in here on the floor?"

"Don't you want to sleep in a bed?" Cindy asked.

"It's more fun. Right Sheeda?" he replied.

"Yeah fun." His little sister giggled. She bounced her butt up and down on the sofa.

"That's fine with me." Cindy said.

After they got their blankets and pillows and spread them out on the floor, Cindy gave them a cup of hot chocolate to drink. Taj pretended to take a couple of sips. He watched Sheeda take a couple of sips and within five minutes she was fast asleep. That was his cue, he laid down and pretended to go to sleep. Cindy turned off everything and went into her room. He laid in the dark wide awake. When he didn't hear any noise or see any light from under her bedroom door, he got up quietly and tiptoed to the front door. He held his breath a second and listened. There was no sound coming from the bedroom. He turned the lock in the doorknob and waited. No noise. He turned the deadbolt lock. No noise. He turned the knob. It was locked. His heart began to beat faster. He slid to the floor and sat with his head in his arms. He was tired and tears were beginning to form in his eyes. They were trapped. He started to crawl back to his blanket and lay down when he remembered that he had forgotten about the lock that required a key. He got back up. There shining in the moonlight was Cindy's pocketbook. Grandma's voice ran through his head. "You're never to go through a woman's pocketbook." This was an emergency. He stuck his hand down in her bag and fished his hand around in there. He felt metal. It was her keys. The mattress springs squeaked from the bedroom. He froze. The noise stopped. He proceeded to tiptoe to the door. There was one small key and two big keys on the key ring. Taj ran his finger over the lock. Big key, he thought. One was a gold key and the other was a silver key on the key ring. The lock was gold so he chose the gold key. It fit the lock.

He turned the key and cracked the door open and slid through the opening. He closed the door carefully and quietly.

Then he ran as fast as he could down the hall looking for the elevator. He hit the button and nervously looked around him. No one was coming. He banged the button "Come on", he said out loud.

The door opened. He selected ground floor. He raced out of the lobby. He started walking towards his house with no coat. It was cold. He passed small groups of people hanging out. He kept walking. Then he saw a pay phone. He pulled some lunch money change that he had been saving to buy candy from the store on the way to school. He didn't want to wake Grandma so he called the only other phone number that he had memorized. He called his big brother, Keith. The phone rang and Keith answered. "Boy, where are you? Everybody is looking for you." Taj didn't really know exactly where he was. He told Keith that he was in Rose Heights Manor, which was the name of the housing project by his house. Keith asked him for the phone number of the pay phone and told him to stay put. Within minutes the pay phone rang and Keith told him that the police were on their way to pick him up and that he would stay on the phone with him until they got there.

Within minutes, the police arrived full of questions. Taj had one question. "Was his Grandmother o.k.?" He was told that she was anxiously waiting at home for him and his little sister. Taj let out a deep breath. "Can you take me to her?" The police told him that as soon as they got his sister, they would be going to Grandma's house. Hearing those words, Taj relaxed and proceeded to tell them everything. When they arrived at Ms. Cindy's building there were enough police cars in sight to make a movie. Taj took the police to Ms Cindy's floor and pointed out her door. He had told them that he had left the door unlocked. Through their line of questioning on the way to the building, he had explained to them who was in the apartment and in which rooms. Taj was ushered downstairs to wait for his sister.

As he walked out of the door, he heard her voice before he saw her. "Taj, come here baby." He turned his head to see his grandmother sitting in the front seat of one of the police cars with her door open and her arms stretched out wide open ready to scoop him up.

"Grandma," he yelled and ran straight into her arms. They hugged and cried. "Grandma, this lady Ms. Cindy brought us here. She told us that you were sick and that you asked her to take care of us."

"Baby, I would never leave you with a stranger."

"I told her that we were supposed to go to Ms. Sadie's but before I could get Sheeda and leave, she gave me something to drink that put me to sleep. I realized that she was crazy. She kept calling me, Henry and she called Sheeda, Sheila."

"That gal is crazy. She must be having a mental breakdown. She lost two of her children in a fire a few years ago." She rocked him in her lap.

"Thank God, you are alright. I'll be glad when they bring Sheeda down here with us." She let out a loud sign and she continued to rock him. "It's gonna be alright baby. It's gonna be alright." Taj was beginning to drift off in her lap when he heard Sheeda's crying. Grandma placed Taj next to her on the front seat as she held her hands out for Sheeda. "Sh Ssh" Grandma said as she held Sheeda in her lap. "It's alright now. It's alright." Sheeda quieted down. "I know. They woke you up out of your sleep. It's all right. Now you can go home and go back to sleep in your bed. You and your brother." Sheeda turned to Taj and grabbed his hand and held it, as she placed the thumb from her free hand in her mouth. Just then Ms. Cindy was brought out of the building in handcuffs.

She glanced over at the car. Taj quickly leaned towards the open door and said, "My grandma is all better now. See?" Cindy looked over at them with a blank look on her face. The policewoman jerked Cindy back towards the direction of the police car.

"That gal used to come to the playground with her baby, Rodney. Sheeda started playing with her baby and we started talking. She was so friendly. I had told her how blessed I was to have you and Sheeda. Her kids death has driven her mad. She stole you from me to replace her dead children." Grandma hugged them at the thought. "Our love will keep us together always."

Momma Harris

"Look Ma! Uncle Butch touched Momma Harris' hand," my cousin Crystal whispered loudly as she waited with her mother in the line of people waiting to look on my grandmother whose casket was in the living room. I could only imagine what her hand must feel like now that she was dead. As I looked down at my own, I thought about her hands. They had always been pleasingly warm to the touch. Her skin was loose to the touch but her grip was always firm. My father was standing in the line with me while my mother kept herself busy in the kitchen.

"Celena, are you okay?" I nodded my head and turned to face forward in the line. Momma Harris looked like she was sleeping. She reminded me of Snow White lying in the glass coffin fast asleep while the dwarfs performed their work around her. Right next to her casket was her rocking chair; which was so appropriate since she never missed a day sitting in that chair until she became too sick to sit up. She told me once if I ever wanted to solve a problem just pray on it, don't dwell on it, forget about it and let the Lord take care of it. The best way to put a problem out of your mind after you pray on it is to rock in your rocking chair until the problem has left your mind. I remembered the first time I saw the power of that rocking chair at work.

"Don't get dirty playing out there. I don't want you dirty when your Ma comes to get you."

"I won't get dirty, Momma Harris. I promise."

"Alright now, you don't want to see me get mad," she said with a little fire under her breath. "How could I get dirty out here? There's nothing but grass and grapevines back here in the yard," I thought to myself. I walked through the grapevines. The grapes smelled like sour berries. I began to run since just past the grapevines were nothing but green grass and the alley. I ran to the back gate. In the alley was one of the bad boys from the neighborhood standing right by Momma Harris' back gate.

"What are you doing back here?" I demanded. I was all of 7 years old. I had heard my grandma, momma and sister use this tone successfully. He ignored my tone.

"I found a dead cat right by your gate. You know they say cats have nine lives. I'm poking at it so that it can come back to life." I looked through the gate to see flies surrounding the matted fur animal. The cat's body was so decomposed, I couldn't tell if it were a cat or a rat. I ran around the yard looking for a stick to help my new friend bring the cat back to life. I had poked at it a few times when I heard Papa walk up right behind me.

"Cee, what you doing back here by the gate?"

"Papa, we're trying to bring the cat back to life," I said real matter of fact like I did this every day. He looked over the gate down at the tormented creature.

"Bringing a cat back to life, huh?" His tone suggested that I didn't know what I was talking about. "Don't you touch that cat with your hands. You don't know if that cat has some disease or something." I stopped poking the cat with the stick. I didn't want Papa to be upset with me. He was my friend. He took me with him whenever he could to show me off to everyone that he knew. I was his daughter; Linda's child, and he would tell everyone that we came across just that when we went walking. He always took up for me when Momma Harris or my Mommy fussed at me.

"Boy, where you live?" Papa asked my alley friend.

"Around the corner," my friend answered.

"Whereabouts round the corner? "

"On Poe Street," the boy answered as he kept on poking at the cat.

"Boy, you a long ways from home. Now you better git on your way before I take you around to your Mama's house myself."

"Come on here gal, you need to be closer to the back door." At the mention of his mother, my friend left. We walked back to the back steps. Papa sat in a chair on the back porch and I sat on the back steps scratching a rock on the concrete step, creating chalk lines. After a few minutes, I looked at Papa. He had fallen fast asleep in the chair.

Momma Harris was standing at the back door, looking in the yard. "Robert, don't just sit there and fall asleep."

"Huh?" He sat up. "Let me get my behind up and do some work round here." He went inside and I wandered through the grapevines. There were bees flying through the vines. I was terrified of bees. I was poking at the grapes that had fallen from the vines when a bumblebee buzzed by my ear. I took off running towards the house hollering and fell right over my feet onto the cement walk right in front of the back steps. Oh the pain. I hollered louder. This pain was nothing compared to the bees.

Momma Harris came to the back door. "I told you not to get dirty." I hollered more. Momma Harris was mad at me now.

"Robert, come git the baby, she fell." I was still hollering cause now Papa was probably going to be mad at me as well.

"Wah, wah. Listen to the baby crying. I thought that we had all big girls round here, Momma."

"Yeah, me too. That's what they told me. Linda said that a big girl was coming to spend the day with us today." Papa picked me up skin, blood and bones and carried me in his arms into the house.

"This here's what I found making all that noise outside, Momma." Momma Harris had a wet washcloth in her hand.

"Humph, bring her in the living room and let me get a better look at her." Momma Harris put on her reading glasses and sat down in her rocking chair with the washcloth still in her hand. Papa laid me in her lap. I had stopped crying by now. Even though my knees burned and they were dirty with blood and dirt, Momma Harris cradled me in her arms as she began to hum. She wiped off my scraped knees and hands and she rocked me right to sleep. When I woke up, I was in her bed and my knees were still a little sore but I felt so much better. The rocking chair had made my problem go away. I was in so much pain at the time, that I didn't have time to pray but God knew what was best in the end as Momma Harris always said.

I was close to the rocking chair now in the viewing line. I decided not to sit in it to rest my feet out of respect to Momma Harris. I was still bothered that Butch had touched her hand. So I did the next best thing for comfort. I rubbed the arm of the rocking chair and said a silent prayer to God for strength to continue living without being able to talk to Momma Harris everyday. I would miss her terribly. I was missing her now. I knew from experience that it would take awhile to get used to not seeing her just like when Papa passed away. I still remember the last time that I saw him.

Momma Harris and Papa knew everybody. They loved to have parties. Papa would always end up embarrassing Momma Harris because he would get drunk. They were going to have a summer party one Saturday. Momma Harris had come over our house earlier in the day and borrowed our card table and some candy dishes. She was dressed up in a sleeveless floral dress and some flower petal earrings with a matching necklace. She was laughing and she was so happy that day. We came to the party that evening. I had on a sleeveless floral dress too. Everyone kept commenting that I looked like a little Momma Harris with that dress on. Later that evening, I danced with my daddy as we competed dancing with another couple. How dare they even think they could beat us. Sure enough based on the cheers, we won.

After I finished dancing with daddy, Papa said "Baby girl, come sit with me." He was beginning to slur in his speech. I was drinking ginger ale out of a plastic champagne glass. You couldn't tell me that I wasn't the princess of the ball that night. It was getting late and I was trying hard to stay awake. "Baby girl, you were showing them old folks a little something tonight. Why don't you and I get out there and show them how it's REALLY done."

I laughed. "I'll be back Papa." I had to go to the bathroom. I noticed a strange thing on the way to the bathroom, Momma Harris chair was rocking by itself.

When I came back, everyone was standing in a big circle around the room. I went up to Papa. His head was leaning to one side of the high back chair as if he were asleep.

"Papa," I touched his hand. "Papa" Nobody came forward. I didn't realize it at the time but everyone was staring at me.

"Joe, get her." I heard Momma Harris say to my daddy.

"Cee, come over here with me." I went to stand with my father.

"Papa's asleep?" I asked.

"No", my father answered. "Papa's sick. The doctor is on his way. Let's get you home. It's been a long night." As Daddy and I got in the car, I saw the ambulance in the middle of the street and two paramedics with a stretcher going into Momma Harris' house to get Papa. He never did recover. He died within a matter of days. A blood vessel in his brain had burst.

After that, Momma Harris sat in her rocking chair a lot. We would go to visit her often and I would tell her that I missed Papa. I didn't have anyone to take up for me anymore when Momma Harris or Mommy was mean to me. When I visited her now, she would pat her lap for me to come and sit with her and we would rock in her chair until we had forgotten our problem. Then, we would talk about school, church or relatives.

The summer after Papa passed, my parents went to a convention and no children were allowed. I was going to stay with Momma Harris. I had never spent the night over her house before. As soon as my parents left us, she read off the rules of her house. The list seemed so long that my head started spinning. A few items were very clear to me. Don't ask for anything to eat unless you really want it. Don't ask to sleep in Momma Harris bed. Only big girls were allowed to stay with her so don't even think about trying no baby stuff. The ultimate rule, there would be no peeing in the bed. If you had to go to the bathroom in the middle of the night, get up and go. Naturally, I signed the contract prematurely. I was too young to know that there were clauses in contracts. Within 4 hours of being there, I found out the first thing that I'd never known about her house. There were squirrels that lived in the walls on one side of her house and birds that lived on the other side of the wall.

I found this out playing in her bedroom while she was on the phone talking to my Aunt Sadie. I heard a scratching sound coming from the walls. Out loud I said, "What's that?"

Momma Harris heard me and immediately whispered. "Those are the squirrels in the wall." You could have told me that the house was on fire. I jumped up and went and sat right next to her on the bed.

"Can't they come through the walls into the house?"

"Yeah, to get you!" My eyes got big. She really got a rise out of my reaction. After she calmed down, she said. "They don't like tough meat. You're a little too tough for their taste. The older you are. The tougher your skin. You don't have anything to worry about." Whew, what a relief. "The birds can't fly in the wall so they aren't going anywhere. You just better hope that the squirrels can't get to them and so far they haven't so I don't think that we have anything to worry about." My mind was spinning. Did she really think that I was going to sleep in another bed in her house after learning all of this information? That night, I asked if I could sleep in her bed. She told me that I could but I couldn't be switching back and forth between rooms. I nodded. I didn't want to make her mad because I didn't want to see the squirrels staring in my face in the middle of the night.

The next morning, she was up when I woke up that morning. I could smell the bacon from downstairs. I came downstairs in my robe. She was in the living room in her chair with Ms. Regina Patterson and a man. They were in the midst of praying. I tiptoed to the kitchen. I saw that the table was set. I went to the frying pan and the bacon was already cooked. I reached for a piece, but before I could get it Momma Harris yelled from the kitchen. "Cee, there will be no eating until prayer is over. Now get your behind in here." I rushed in the living room and sat down in the first chair that I saw, which happened to be next to the strange man. His clothes were dirty and his hair needed combing. Momma introduced me to Spurlock.

He smiled a crooked smile and said "Hi Horsy". I laughed. Momma Harris and Ms. Regina laughed too.

"Why you call my granddaughter, Horsy?" She looked offended but she didn't sound upset.

"She reminds me of the cute little ponies at the track. They have thick tails and that's what her two plaits look like." He paused like he had to burp.

"Two thick horse tails." Grandma started rocking fast. "You trying to tell me that my baby's plaits remind you of a horse's ass?" She didn't say the last word. She just mouthed it silently.

Ms. Regina laughed. "Look here, I need to get ready to go."

"Okay Cee, go set a place at the table for Spurlock. He's staying for breakfast this morning."

I wasn't hungry after I watched Spurlock eat. Now that was what you called a hungry man. From the time the plate of food was placed in front of him until there was no more food left on his plate, he kept his head down shoveling food into his mouth. I had just started eating when he dropped his fork on the plate.

"Miz Harris, you my savior. I spend all day trying to get a job so that I can buy some food but won't nobody hire me or give me nothing to eat. Horsy, don't let nobody tell you different. Your grandma is a saint." He starting sniffling real loud and before I knew it he was crying. Momma Harris took it all in stride. She got up calmly handed him a tissue and a brown paper bag with food in it. He calmed down as she walked him to the door.

"Now do like I told you. Go down to Harvey's Market. Tell them that I sent you. They need a worker down there." She let him out and came back and ate the rest of her breakfast in silence. During the rest of my stay, I learned that Momma Harris lived her life with her bible by her side and in her rocking chair. She woke in the morning and read the bible and prayed in her chair. She took her nap during the day in her chair. She listened to the news after dinner in her chair. Most important if anyone came to see her for advice, you could tell which way she was going to decide by how she rocked in her chair.

My Aunt Gladys had put my cousin Scotty out of the house. He didn't have anywhere to go so he came to see Momma Harris. She and I had just finished listening to the news when Scotty rang the doorbell. I was glad to see another younger person. I had been dealing with old people all week. Momma Harris didn't look too happy to see him. Scotty was funny. He always said something funny that made you laugh. I couldn't figure out why Momma Harris wasn't glad to see him. She sat down in her chair. "Momma, I know that my Mumma has probably already called you." Momma Harris didn't say a word. She just stared at him and slowly rocked in her chair. "Anyhow, I need some place to stay. My Mumma put me out because I came home drunk late last night. We got in an argument and I picked up a lamp and threw it at the wall." Momma's rocking had picked up a whole lot of speed now.

Scotty kept talking. "I know that I was wrong. I apologized but the damage had already been done."

Momma stopped rocking. "Boy, you got a whole lot of nerve coming over here after you done threw a lamp at my daughter. I ought to call the police and have you arrested for such foolishness." She was pointing her finger at him.

"Momma, you know me. I been working and I just went out to have a little fun last night."

She was rocking fast again. "I don't care what you did last night. But I tell you one thing. You lost your flippin' head last night. God is good." She stopped rocking and raised her hand and looked up to the ceiling. "Cause if you was one of my children, I swear to God, I would have knocked your teeth down your throat last night. Now bout staying here, I ain't taking none of your mess. If you even raise a finger to me, I'll kill you. Now try me if you want. I ain't worried." By the time

Momma Harris finished with Scotty, he was sweating. But she on the other hand was cool as a cucumber and she had a nice steady rocking rhythm with her chair.

I was glad Momma Harris let Scotty stay. When he came home from work, he would take me to the playground. I wasn't allowed to walk there by myself. He would meet his friends there while I played. By the time, my parents came to pick me up, I was as straight as an arrow and I had learned quite a bit about life. It was boring at my house compared to the comings and goings at Momma's. I cried when I had to leave. Momma Harris was looking tough. "There you go. As soon as your mommy and daddy get here, you start acting like a baby. Where is the big girl that spent the last two weeks with me?" I wiped my tears away.

"Right here." I pointed at me.

"That's right." She smiled. "Now come on let's pack up your stuff while your parents talk to Scotty." While we were packing my things, Momma Harris whispered, "You can come back anytime now you hear, as long as you leave that baby mess at home." I hugged and kissed her.

True to Momma Harris' word, if I asked my parents to let me go and visit, she would let me come over. One morning, I was putting breakfast on the table for us. She was sitting in her rocking chair. I called her and told her that breakfast was ready. She didn't come. I went to check on her and she was slumped over in her chair. I ran next door to her neighbor's house for help. The doctor told us that Momma Harris was really sick. Aunt Gladys moved in with her and her bed was moved into the living room with her chair right next to it. I would go visit Momma Harris at least once a week and we would talk about school. One day when I came to visit Momma Harris, she slept the entire time. Aunt Gladys said that she was in a coma. "What's that?"

"Baby, Momma Harris is in a deep sleep."

"When will she wake up?"

"Baby, we don't know but the doctor said that it's good to talk to her. She might hear you and wake up." I still continued to come see Momma Harris even though she was sleeping all the time. I would tell her about my day. Even though she was asleep, her chair would rock from the time that I started talking until the time that I finished.

One day, I came to see her and she was wide-awake. She smiled when she saw me. The entire family came to see Momma Harris that day. It was like Christmas. Everyone told her what they had been doing. She just smiled and said "I know. I've been listening to you even though I couldn't tell you. I just want you all to know that I love each and every one of you. We will be together again one day." She died in her sleep that night and her chair rocked all night.

"I miss you Momma Harris." I said to her sleeping form in the casket as we paid our respects.

The night of her funeral there was a terrible thunderstorm and her rocking chair rocked all night. This scared Aunt Gladys. She said that Momma Harris' presence could be felt in the house. "Fine by me." I thought. When I needed advice, I knew where to go. A girl was picking on me at school and I didn't for the life of me know why. After all, I had done nothing to this girl. "Should I just tell the girl to leave me alone?" I asked my Momma's chair. It didn't move. "Should I confront her and ask her why and then tell her to leave me alone?" The chair rocked slightly. I knew what to do. I confronted Melody the next day and asked her why she was bothering me since I never bothered her? Before she could answer, I told her that she had messed with me for the last time. She just stared at me and went back to playing on the jungle gym and never bothered me again.

When Tyrone embarrassed me by kissing me in front of everyone on the schoolyard, I was bewildered to say the least. He was ugly. He had frog lips. Plus he was telling everyone that he was my boyfriend. When I denied it, everyone just laughed and said, "Sure." Like they didn't believe me.

I went to Momma's house. I needed advice. But the chair was gone. I ran through the house and found Scotty. "Where is Momma's chair?" I was beside myself.

"Mumma had it sent to the Salvation Army."

"WHAT?"

"She was scared of the chair anyway and so was I. There were times when we would walk into the living room and the chair would be rocking by itself and it was really bad at night it was getting to the point that we were scared to sleep some nights cause we would hear the chair rocking loud downstairs and we knew that no one was downstairs cause we would be in the bed. Mumma swore that the chair was haunted and she said Momma Harris was probably mad that we were living in her house." I didn't even hear the end of his sentence. I went outside and sat on the back step looking at the grapevines. What was I going to do? I couldn't talk to Momma Harris anymore. Tears sprang to my eyes. I missed her so bad. I could tell her things that nobody else understood and she would always understand and tell me what I should do. I cried like a newborn on the back steps. When I didn't have another tear to spare, I stared at the grapevines. I knew that I wouldn't be back over here again. Aunt Gladys was a cussing alcoholic. I can't say that she didn't get it honest when I thought about Papa. She definitely wasn't my kind of folks and boy was she lazy. Scotty couldn't help getting drunk. He was just trying to act like his Mumma. There was nothing left in the house for me to visit. But you know what I'm Momma and Papa's grandchild. They taught me a lot and I still remembered all their rules and lessons. I just needed to write them now before I forgot them so that I could share them with my kids one day. They are still with me even though I can't see them. I just need to get quiet and still and listen inside me and they are there. As I sat quiet and still watching the bumblebees flying around the grapevines, I listened to Momma Harris tell me what to do about Tyrone.

ORDER FORM

Orders can be placed by fax: 443-583-0275
or by mail order form to:
SaySo Publishing Co.
P.O. Box 1301
Columbia, MD 21044

NAME	
ADDRESS	
CITY	
STATE	
ZIP	

Qty.	Title	Price
_____	Urban Fairytales	$14.95
	MD tax 5%	$_____
	Priority Mail Shipping	$3.85
	Handling	$1.50
	Total	$_____

(Checks and money orders accepted.)

Orders may also be placed online by visiting www.saysopublishing.com
or by e-mailing us at saysopublishing@aol.com